A
TREASURE
TO DIE FOR

BOOKS BY TERRY AMBROSE

McKenna Mysteries
PHOTO FINISH
KAUAI TEMPTATIONS
BIG ISLAND BLUES
MYSTERY OF THE LEI PALAOA
HONOLULU HOTTIE
NORTH SHORE NANNY
A DAMSEL FOR SANTA
MAUI MAGIC

License to Lie Series
LICENSE TO LIE
CON GAME

A Lei Crime Kindle World
TOUGH CHOICES
STEALING HONOLULU

Anthologies with Stories
PARADISE, PASSION, MURDER: 10 TALES OF MYSTERY
FROM HAWAI'I
HAPPY HOMICIDES 3: SUMMERTIME CRIMES
HAPPY HOMICIDES 4: FALL INTO CRIME
HAPPY HOMICIDES 5: THE PURR-FECT CRIME
HAPPY HOMICIDES 6: COOKING UP CRIME

A TREASURE TO DIE FOR

A Seaside Cove
Bed & Breakfast Mystery

TERRY AMBROSE

A TREASURE TO DIE FOR

A Seasisde Cove
Bed & Breakfast Mystery

ISBN: 978-0-9964282-2-4

Cover design by Dar Albert

Book design by Pen 2 Ink Designs and is reproduced by permission.

DEDICATION

To Cynthia Jo
May your light burn forever bright.

1

ALEX

June 15

Hey Journal—

We have a real Indiana Jones staying at the B&B!

This is my first entry since I got you for my birthday. I didn't write sooner cause I couldn't think of how to start. But this is so awesome. A whole group of people looking for sunken treasure are coming in today. The man who got here first said they found a map to where an old ship sank. This is totally cool and I just gotta tell somebody.

Daddy was happy cause we're full up for the weekend. I got to check people in cause he was helping the first ones with their bags. I know that sounds kinda boring, but now that I'm ten, I'm supposed to help out more. Guess that means I got my first job. Isn't that awesome, Journal?

Should I call you Journal? Maybe Diary? I'll ask Marquetta cause she'll know. I kinda get why she gave you to me. This is fun. Daddy's gonna be on his way up soon to tuck me in, so I gotta go.

Bye for now,

Alexandra Atwood

PS I guess I don't have to sign every note I put in here, but my first one feels kinda special.

2

RICK

A blast of heat hit Rick Atwood in the face as he opened the oven door and eyed Marquetta's two loaves of Fresh Apple Bread. The heavenly aroma of baking apples, cinnamon, and nutmeg wafted up to greet him. The interior oven light reflected off the browned tops of both loaves. His mouth watered, but he shrugged off the urge to jab a fork into the loaf and taste test a mouthful of heaven in a pan. He placed each loaf on a separate cooling rack, picked up Marquetta's cake tester—a piece of metal that resembled a long toothpick—and tested each crusty loaf.

"Okay, no gooey batter. Only a couple of crumbs on this... miniature spear," he said. "That means they're done?"

Marquetta rolled her eyes and snickered. "That's one of my favorite tools. Don't be insulting it. Yes, they're done. Leave them on the cooling racks for ten minutes."

Rick nodded. "Got it. I can't believe you were able to throw this together on such short notice." He lowered his voice. "These treasure hunters, can you believe it? I hope they're not all like this Jim Gordon. He's a real jerk."

"Be happy they're here, Rick. At least we're full for the weekend." Marquetta returned to the stove and flipped one of the eggs frying in a heavy skillet. "Besides, last-minute requests are my specialty. It's comforting knowing all that cooking school Captain Jack paid for is going to good use."

Rick looked around the kitchen. The B&B had so many little mysteries of its own. This was much more elegant than most B&Bs, thanks to the remodel Rick's grandfather did ten years ago. From the six-burner, stainless steel stove to the refrigerator with French doors, everything was top of the line. Even Marquetta's set of Demeyere pots and pans, which hung from the copper rack above the center island, gleamed in their perfection. The remodel had cost a small fortune—actually, a rather substantial one. As had sending an eighteen-year-old girl to San Francisco so she could become a chef.

The day Rick and Alex moved to Seaside Cove, he began hearing about his grandfather. Captain Jack. World War II Navy Captain. Ran a tight ship to his dying day. Why he'd sent Marquetta to a top culinary arts school in San Francisco, Rick might never know. One possibility was that the old man was a sucker for a pretty face. The rumors flew about town and Rick marveled at how much—and how little—people really knew about the man who bequeathed him the B&B.

Rick set down his oven mitts and stood next to Alex. He drained the last of the coffee from his Seaside Cove Bed & Breakfast mug and gave his daughter's shoulder a gentle squeeze. "What's up, kiddo?"

Alex looked up from the bowl of cereal she'd been munching on. "I think it's awesome, Daddy. Mr. Gordon was nice to me. He even told me he'd let me see the treasure when they brought it up." She reached for her juice glass. "So what am I supposed to do today? You said now that summer's here you want me to help out more."

"I do. I'm thinking you can work with Marquetta." Rick winced. He'd forgotten to ask Marquetta if she was willing to take on a helper today. He snuck a peek at the woman who served as cook, maid, and occasional babysitter.

She was looking directly at him, her head cocked to one side, one eyebrow arched.

"If that's okay with you," he added.

Marquetta's face lit up. "I'd love to have a helper." She turned back to the stove, flipped two more eggs, and wrapped a paper towel around the bacon. When she'd finished, she grabbed her own mug, raised it to her lips, and winked at Alex. "You can start right after you finish your breakfast, Sweetie. We'll have fun working together. I'll take you shopping this afternoon. We're getting low on a few essentials."

Alex beamed at her. "Awesome."

"Eggs are done. One hard, two over easy. You're up, Rick." Marquetta turned off the heat on the burner, slid the eggs and bacon onto a couple of plates with a spatula, and handed them to Rick. "Right hand is for Miss Potok; the left is for Mr. Kalstone. Now, I need to get a grocery list going for this afternoon."

"Aye, aye, sir." Rick nodded at Marquetta as he backed through the butler door leading to the dining room.

Five of the eight guests booked for the weekend had checked in on Friday. There were three more arriving later today. The man who organized the weekend, Jim Gordon, had been the first to arrive. Monica Clark-Kelley, Reese Potok, Cadman Richardson, and Hayden Kalstone soon followed. Those four were seated together for breakfast and, to Rick's surprise, Jim Gordon was nowhere to be found. Apparently, the group had been having quite the discussion about their missing leader.

"Jim's always been a jerk," Cadman said. "I learned that when he stole my shoe design."

Monica Clark-Kelley picked up her coffee cup and gazed at Cadman over the rim. "Look, we all know how Jim is. But, he did organize this weekend so we can all find the *San Manuel* together. Maybe he's trying to make amends."

Rick went first to Reese Potok and waited for her to shift to her right. He laid the plate in front of her while she continued scribbling notes on the pad of paper at her side. He glanced down.

Impressive. Perfectly formed, smooth letters. She'd clipped a small square of paper on which there were squiggly lines to her notes. The attachment reminded Rick of a small section from a topographic map.

She acknowledged Rick with a whispered, "Thank you," before she returned to writing.

"You're welcome," Rick whispered. He walked around the table to deliver Hayden Kalstone's plate.

"It is curious," the man said as Rick put the plate in front of him. The moment Rick pulled his hand away, Hayden repositioned it with the eggs closest and the potatoes farthest away. He also straightened his silverware and placed his napkin on his lap. He barely glanced at Rick as he handed him his mug. "More coffee."

"Jeez, Hayden, you could at least say please," Monica said.

Hayden cocked his head to one side and gazed at her. "Why? It's his job."

It hadn't taken a genius to figure out right away that this guy was a "one-star reviewer." He was the kind who saw no need to compliment good service, but always had a reason to complain. "Of course," Rick said pleasantly.

Monica shook her head ever so slightly and glanced at Reese, who shrugged. "That's Hayden, Monica. He's our very own Mr. Spock." She chuckled as she looked up at Rick. "I'd appreciate another cup, too. Please?"

"My pleasure."

Rick acknowledged Reese with a wink. It surprised him when she glanced away and immediately let her gaze flick back to his. She had a beautiful smile. An attractive young woman. He returned to the kitchen and found Alex finishing up the last of her cereal.

"Marquetta, who's drinking what?" Rick asked as he held up both carafes.

"Mr. Kalstone has decaf, the others have leaded. Mr. Kalstone is quite particular, Rick. When you pour, be sure to do it well away from him. He doesn't want a stray drop to stain his clothes."

Rick eyed Marquetta for a second. When he got no response he asked, "Are you serious?"

She nodded and whispered to him. "He's a strange duck."

Upon returning to the dining room, Rick poured the decaf first, then started refilling the others' cups. When he got to Monica, he noticed another scrap of paper like the one Reese had. When she looked up to thank him, Rick said, "You have one, too."

She picked up the three-inch by three-inch square of paper. "It's part of a treasure map. It's why we're all here. Except for Cadman, of course. He'd forget his head if it wasn't attached, so he has no idea why he's here."

"I have Delayed Memory Syndrome," Cadman said as he feigned indignation, then chuckled.

A series of snickers made their way round the table.

Rick glanced at the map section and the envelope beneath it. It was similar to those used for wedding or party invitations and the address was familiar, but not overly so. Where had he seen it? "You've come prepared," he said.

Hayden sat perfectly erect in his chair and spoke in a firm voice. "Our instructions were quite explicit, Monica. We should not discuss this with outsiders."

"Oh, pooh. Pooh on Jim Gordon's instructions. What's Rick going to do, arrange an expedition in the next ten minutes? I don't think so. Besides, there are three more coming today and they've all got a part of the map, too." She glanced up at Rick. "As you can tell, Hayden is a rather by-the-book kind of guy. The rest of us are more laid back."

Reese giggled. "Please, ignore Hayden. We all do."

"No worries," Rick said as he gazed across the table at her. "We have a lot of treasure seekers around here, but I've never heard of the *San Manuel*."

"Unlike most of the amateurs, we have a reliable map." Reese winked at him. "We also have lots of enthusiasm."

"Anyway, that's my contribution to this weekend," Monica said as she laid down the little square of paper.

"Well, good luck with it. How exciting." Rick scanned the faces around the table. "Can I get anyone anything else?"

Heads shook, then Cadman leaned back in his chair. "I'm stumped as to why Jim would include us in this venture. Unfortunately, he has the 'X marks the spot' part of the map, so I guess we're stuck with him. Where the devil is he, anyway?"

3

RICK

By 8:30, the guests were done with breakfast and the dining room was empty. Marquetta and Alex were finishing the last of the cleanup, so Rick went in search of Jim Gordon. He found him in one of the Adirondack chairs on the patio gazing beyond the old Douglas fir trees to the rocky shore and ocean. In the distance, the Seaside Cove lighthouse still stood. Though it hadn't been active for many years, the structure still drew attention from painters, photographers, and sightseers.

When Rick approached, Gordon acknowledged him with a grunt and continued sipping his coffee.

"Mr. Gordon, can I ask you a question?"

"Sure. Why not? Everybody wants a piece of me today. That's why I skipped breakfast." He rolled his eyes and huffed while he continued to watch the distant waves.

"Yes, I'm sorry you missed the apple bread Marquetta made. The others ate all of it. She can't make more until after we get to the store later today."

"What of it?"

"Nothing, really. Since you put in the special request, I thought you should know."

Gordon fixed an icy stare on Rick. "I had other things on my mind."

Why was he being such a jerk? Rick kept his voice level. "Right. Well, anyway, if you don't mind my asking, why did you invite all your friends if you didn't want this weekend to happen?"

"First off, these people aren't my friends," he snapped. "Second, I didn't invite them. I'm almost positive it's Cadman. He's been screwing with me since he quit the business. And, third, speaking of business, it's none of yours." Gordon stood and handed Rick his empty mug. "Why don't you run along and make sure everything is set up for later today. Apparently, I've got more 'friends' coming in and I intend to find out who arranged this whole fiasco."

"Cadman seems like a decent guy. You could ask him what he knows," Rick snapped. He winced and quickly apologized. "That was uncalled for. You're right, it's none of my business."

Gordon smiled for the first time. "It's okay. They tell me I have a way of bringing out the worst in people. Don't worry about it. Anyway, Cadman would deny he set this up. When I do find out who's behind it, I'm going to kill them." He paused and laughed. "That was a joke. Anyway, I found the *San Manuel* all on my own and I don't intend to share that treasure with any of these slackers. And that includes my ex-business partner."

Rick watched as Gordon followed the pathway to the house. He opened the French door, started to enter, but stepped aside to let Monica out. She moved closer and rubbed his shoulder with her hand, which left Rick wondering how friendly these two were. This looked like a lot more than something platonic. The mood ended a second later when Gordon brushed off her hand and pushed by her. He went inside, left the door standing open, and Monica by herself. She turned, saw Rick, and quickly averted her gaze. She then did an abrupt about-face and ducked through the open door. Rick fingered his earlobe and sighed as he thought about what he'd heard this morning.

The conversation with Gordon had reminded Rick where he'd seen the return address on Monica's envelope. It was Jim

Gordon's. At least, it was the address on his registration. So if he had issued the invitations, why was he denying his role as the event organizer? And now this thing with Monica. Strange man. Even though he'd cracked and shown he did have feelings, the way he acted made it nearly impossible for Rick to like him.

Rick took a last look at the waves crashing against the rock-lined shore. Further out, little bands of white dotted the undulating waves. And there, at the westernmost tip of the bay, stood the lighthouse. Rick breathed deeply, took in the salty air, and shook off Gordon's foul-mood contagion. Gordon's mug in hand, he walked into the kitchen where he found Marquetta finishing her grocery list.

She smiled at him and whispered, "He's a very insulting man, isn't he?"

Rick rinsed the mug, set it in the sink, and kept his voice low as he spoke. "He has a way of making you feel about this tall." He raised his hand with his thumb and index finger spread about two inches apart. "But he did smile when I snapped at him. By the way, why are we whispering?"

They laughed together and Marquetta shrugged. "No idea. We've got another problem. I have to prepare the appetizers for this afternoon's welcome session, but one of the guests spilled orange juice on the area rug in the dining room."

"You've got to be kidding me. We just had that cleaned."

"I took a look, and it's not too bad. If I get on it right away, I can take care of it before I start the food prep. We've got most of what we need, so if you could do the grocery shopping with Alex, it would save me a huge amount of time."

"Sure, no problem. Actually, she wanted to go for ice cream today. I should be working on the books, but I have a couple of hours. We'll get the groceries first, then pay a visit to Scoops & Scones on the way back. Will that work?"

Marquetta ran her tongue across her lower lip as she examined the list. Rick studied her. With her girl-next-door brown hair and gray eyes she reminded him of a grade-school Valentine—the complete opposite of his...what was Giselle? She wasn't his ex-wife—they were still married. Nevertheless, they hadn't seen each other since he and Alex moved here.

"What's wrong, Rick?"

Other than he'd married at eighteen, his relationship with Giselle was a catastrophe, and he didn't know whether to cling to the past or move on? He shook his head. "Nothing. Just thinking how lucky I am you stayed after I inherited this place."

"That you are, boss." Marquetta brushed back a strand of hair and winked at him. "Tell you what. Take your daughter and have some fun. You two deserve it because we're in for a hectic weekend."

4

ALEX

June 16

Hey Journal—

I gotta tell this to someone cause I'm about ready to burst. I can't tell Marquetta cause she'll tell Daddy. And I don't want him to know it's about him. Marquetta says everybody has stuff they're hiding, so I don't feel too guilty. But it makes me super sad cause I ruined my dad's life.

He always says it wasn't cause of me that Mom left us. It was because she wanted to be a big actress in New York and we didn't fit into her plans. But they were happy before they had me. Daddy's told me how good it was right after they got married. He's lonely here in Seaside Cove and it has to be my fault. That's why I gotta fix the problem.

If Daddy didn't have to worry about me, he'd still be in New York with my mom. He says we can't go back, so I gotta find a way to make him happy again. If he had a girlfriend things would be better. I wanna go to Mrs. Carter's shop today cause her daughter Bella is coming home in a few weeks. That's what Marquetta told me. Since I can't go that far by myself, I fibbed and said I wanted ice cream.

Marquetta says Mrs. Carter is trying to marry Bella off. I saw a picture of her in the shop a couple months ago. She's pretty. I asked Marquetta about her one time and she said Bella wasn't a busybody like her mom. I think that's good, right?

Anyway, I feel better cause I wrote this down. I hope I can make Daddy happy again.

Bye for now,

Alex

PS I gotta remember to ask Marquetta if I should be signing this or not.

5

RICK

The brass bell attached to the door clanged as Rick and Alex entered Francine Carter's ice cream shop, Scoops & Scones. Upon moving to town, Rick had discovered that many of the local stores had similarly quaint names. He'd also noticed a distinct lack of chains and franchises. Everything in this town was purely local.

On several occasions, Francine had reminded Rick this was no ordinary front door bell, but one once owned by Thomas Jefferson himself. The bell had passed through nine generations of Carters, and it was Francine's sincere hope her daughter would carry on the tradition. The story was usually followed by a not-so-subtle hint that, under the right circumstances, the bell could wind up in Rick's family.

"Hello, Rick." Never one to miss an opportunity to shape public opinion, Francine immediately unleashed her charms on Alex. "And how are you today, dear?"

"I'm good."

Francine smiled at her, then turned back to Rick. "That's quite a group of treasure hunters you have staying this weekend. Are there more coming?"

Well, that was a surprise. Francine actually had something other than Bella's future on her mind. He said, "The first five checked in yesterday, three more came in this morning."

"Oh, my." Francine patted the back of her curls. "There could be so many more flocking to us. This is wonderful."

"Yes, it could be good for everyone."

"You know, the town council is discussing how we might capitalize more on all these opportunities. After all, if we could publicize how much lost gold there is around—between the sunken ships coming down from San Francisco to those Joaquin Murrieta tales—oh my goodness, Seaside Cove has tremendous potential. Don't you think?"

"It's awesome." Alex was leaning against Rick's side, apparently having forgotten all about the dessert cravings she'd been talking about all day. "All that treasure! And they're all staying with us. I wanna be a treasure hunter when I grow up."

"Let's work on sixth grade first, okay?" Rick gave Alex's shoulder a playful nudge.

"Okay," she chirped, "but these days you gotta plan ahead, Daddy. Right, Mrs. Carter?" Alex left Rick's side to inspect a photograph hanging on the wall.

Francine smiled sweetly. "You are absolutely correct. Do you know who took that?"

"The little card at the bottom says Bella Carter."

"Yes, and she will be home from college soon. She'd love to see both of you again."

Again? They'd met one time. Here. In this store. The encounter had been short, and Rick doubted if Bella even remembered him. Or Alex. "She's probably got friends she'll want to hang out with during her vacation."

"Don't be silly." Francine trilled like a happy skylark. "We simply must make plans."

Alex wandered over to Homer the Turtle's eighty-gallon tank. She appeared to be ignoring the adult conversation, and that's when Rick finally got it. The reason they were here had nothing to do with ice cream.

He scrunched up his cheek and did his best to look apologetic. "Our calendars are pretty full these days. Besides, we need to get back to our guests." He raised the grocery bag in his arms as a reminder.

Francine's eyes and lips rounded. "Oh, I really must talk to you about two of them." She paused before glancing in Alex's direction.

"What about them?" Rick asked.

"They had quite the altercation. Mr. Gordon and Mr. Richardson. They practically came to blows." She pointed to the sidewalk. "Right there. Just outside my store."

Why hadn't he heard this before? Rick hated the idea of discussing something akin to a street fight in Seaside Cove even though Alex looked to be enthralled with Homer. "I'd prefer to discuss this when Alex isn't around."

Francine screwed up her face and gave him a firm nod as her eyes cut toward the fish tank. "I understand. Children are so malleable at that age. But, you simply must find a solution. The animosity between those two men is absolutely palpable."

Alex beamed as she turned away from the tank. "Homer's happy today."

"Yes, dear, he is." Francine gave the girl another condescending smile.

"Alex, let's get your ice cream," Rick said.

"Does Homer ever get lonely?"

"I don't think so, dear. He is, after all, merely a turtle. Why do you ask?"

"So turtles don't have feelings like people?"

Rick glared at his daughter. He'd guessed correctly. This outing was all about a little girl playing matchmaker. "Sometimes, people need time alone, Alex." He mirrored one of Francine's standard mayoral smiles. "You agree. Right, Francine?"

But, before she could answer, Alex changed the topic by pointing to a sunset photo hanging above Homer's tank. "Was that taken here?"

"Bella took it just last month. I love the way she captured the oranges, reds, and grays. She's quite talented, isn't she? And, Rick, she'll be here for an entire week. You should join us for a small *soirée*. Bella would be delighted."

Great. Here they went again. Round 2. Rick's jaw tightened at the mere thought of an evening with Francine. "I'm sure she'd rather spend time catching up with you and her friends."

Alex shifted her bag of groceries and shook her head. "Daddy, I think it's nice Mrs. Carter wants us to come over. We don't ever do much since we moved here."

"It's going to be busy at the B&B," he snapped. "We have to have coverage and Marquetta might need a day or two off."

"Nonsense," Francine scoffed. "I'll clear it with Marquetta. I'm sure she'll be quite willing to cover for you. It's the least she can do."

"Let's see how Bella feels about it." Rick cleared his throat. "Besides, you'll only have one week together and you're bound to want some mother-daughter time with her."

He tried to let his gaze telegraph the message that he was not happy with Alex, but she ignored him and continued to inspect the artwork.

"I'm sorry to have disturbed you, Francine. It appears my daughter didn't want anything after all."

"No! I do."

"Then you'd better order." He was tired of this ambush. When had his little girl turned into such a con artist?

Francine leaned against the counter and craned her neck toward Alex. "The usual?"

"Yes, please. A double scoop. Tell us about the fight!"

"Single," Rick snapped. "In a cup. No cone."

Alex shrugged and gazed up at Francine. "So what happened?"

"Since when are you so interested in physical violence, Alex?"

Her answer was an exaggerated eye roll. It must mean he was clueless because one look told him there was genuine interest on her face. Now he was really trapped. How was he going to escape without losing the rest of the afternoon?

"Well." Francine emphasized the word, indulged herself by slowly taking in her audience of two, then began. "It started when Mr. Gordon ran into that nasty Mr. Richardson. Apparently, Mr. Richardson organized this weekend with all those guests you have and now he's denying that he did it. His entire claim of innocence sounded extremely weak to me." She paused and let her gaze fall on Alex.

So Gordon had confronted Cadman Richardson after all? Rick wasn't about to reveal his conversation on the patio with Gordon. No way. Francine would spread the word like the gospel on Sunday morning.

When asked if he wanted a scoop of his own, Rick declined, which earned him a disapproving glance but nothing more. She handed a cup and spoon to Alex while prattling on. "From the way they were yelling at each other, you'd think they were launching a mission to Mars. I was certain their disagreement would turn physical, so I called Deputy Cunningham on his personal cell phone. I told him to get over here tout de suite."

"What's toot sweets mean?" Alex asked as she dug into the chocolate with her spoon.

"You'll have to work on the pronunciation a bit, dear, but it's mayor talk for right this instant." Francine glanced up and winked. "She's so adorable. Alex, would you like to visit with Bella when she comes home?"

"Sure, Mrs. Carter."

"It's not a good idea, Francine." Rick held the woman's gaze until she shrugged.

"If that's your parental opinion."

Francine sounded miffed, but Rick didn't care. "Perhaps if I need a babysitter, but Alex is too young to have friends of college age."

Alex's lack of a protest wasn't surprising. Apparently, she had no personal interest in Bella other than her potential role as a romantic lead in this drama Rick called a life. He caught a sudden change in Francine's demeanor and felt his pulse quicken. What was coming next?

"Speaking of older women, you never have said what happened to your wife." Francine once again patted her coiffed hair as she gave him her best mayoral smile.

He wasn't about to discuss Giselle in the presence Francine, either. The woman mainlined gossip like a junkie did cocaine. She was a master at the art of keeping her prey off balance and had three topics he knew of—how many more were in her arsenal?

There was only one way out.

The desperation move.

The long pass. He needed a Hail Mary. What did he have to lose?

Rick leaned forward, lowered his voice to a conspiratorial level, and said, "Francine, they're not arguing over the invitations. That argument was all about sunken treasure. Let me tell you about the legend of the *San Manuel*."

6

RICK

"In 1582, a young sea captain anxious to show his worth to King Philip II of Spain recruited an inexperienced crew to transport Incan gold to Manila."

Rick watched as Francine leaned closer, hanging on his every word. Alex, too, seemed eager to hear the story. He had to make this good. Close enough to what he'd heard from his guests to be plausible, detailed enough to capture Francine's interest. "You're probably aware that navigation wasn't anywhere close to today's standards. For instance, those sailors had nothing like your topographic map on the wall."

Francine and Alex both turned their heads and gazed to the map of the bay Rick had indicated. He wanted to burst out laughing, but instead continued. "So this captain—oh, I wish I could remember this name—in any case, he had a Dutch navigator who had made two previous Manila sailings and whose role was to protect the interests of the financiers of the project." Rick lowered his voice. "The financiers were Dutch merchants and from what we've discovered he may have been a less than honest man. Quite possibly he had decided he was tired of risking his life as a seaman when he might earn more money on land, if you know what I mean. Rumor has it he was looking for early retirement."

"Oh, my," Francine whispered.

Alex no longer paid attention to her ice cream, but watched Rick eagerly.

"So, the experienced navigator and the eager young captain left the port of Acapulco despite an approaching hurricane. Now, Alex, you probably don't know this, but I'm sure Francine does. Tropical cyclones in the Northern Hemisphere rotate counter-clockwise, but it's the opposite below the equator."

"Oh—yes, of course." Francine patted the back of her hair and fanned herself with one hand.

"Mrs. Carter? Are you going through the change?"

Rick nearly choked. "Alex! That's an inappropriate question."

Francine cleared her throat. "It's a little warm in here, dear."

"Alex, apologize to Mrs. Carter."

"I'm sorry," Alex said, then she looked up at Rick. "What did I do, Daddy?"

Before he could answer, Francine said, "Nothing, dear. You'll be studying the subject in school soon enough." She straightened up and put her shoulders back. Her face flushed, and she fanned herself again as she stared at the far wall where another of Bella's landscape photographs predominated. This one was of the Seaside Cove lighthouse. "Don't stop now, what happened to the *San Manuel*? Did they sink here? Near Seaside Cove?"

"That's what Jim Gordon and his band of treasure hunters think. They have a map showing the location. I guess this is sort of an organizational meeting. Who knows, they might be mounting a major expedition out of Seaside Cove in the future."

Francine's hand went to her chest, and she sucked in a slow breath. "That would be wonderful for the town. Can you imagine all the tourists, the workers…the additional tax revenue."

"Yes," Rick nodded. "That would be good for all of us." Had he laid it on too thick? "It's not a sure thing, Francine."

"Oh, by the way, speaking of people coming to town, were you aware that Bella graduates from Wharton next year? She took that lighthouse picture, of course. And that magnificent sunset everyone likes so much."

What? He'd spun that big yarn, and she'd still come back to her daughter? This couldn't be happening. Unable to come up with a better answer, he said, "I believe you have told me that before."

"Oh. I'm just so proud of her. What night should we have you and Alex come for dinner? You'd like that, wouldn't you, dear?" Francine smiled at Alex over the counter.

"Ur-fect!" Alex blurted through a mouthful of chocolate.

Rick felt his temperature rising. These two had tag teamed him. Just when he thought he'd gotten away unscathed. "No talking with your mouth full," he snapped.

Despite the spoon, Alex had chocolate everywhere and Rick had a burning desire to clean her up with a wet napkin. But, the last time he did that, he was the one who received the scolding. It appeared that, as of age ten, Alex considered herself All Grown Up. Well, so be it. Tonight at bedtime, he and his daughter were having an adult-sized talk about priorities. Specifically, his, which did not include marriage for the foreseeable future.

"Shall we say Wednesday night—two weeks hence, perhaps, seven-ish?"

Not. Happening. Rick sighed and hoped it came off as disappointment, not exasperation. "I don't know, Francine we're swamped with these treasure hunters right now."

"Oh, nonsense. Your guests will be gone after the weekend. And your daughter needs a good, home-cooked meal. I doubt if Marquetta is making sure she is fed properly."

"Argeta..."

"Alex! What did I tell you?"

Alex paused, swallowed, and said, "Sorry. But..."

"Finish your ice cream."

Francine's eyes sparkled, and Rick suspected it was the same look a lion had immediately before pouncing on a gazelle.

It wouldn't surprise him if the mayor hadn't already picked out a ring.

This was a losing battle. His diversionary tactic had failed, so his best option was to beat a hasty retreat. "Maybe at some point when things settle down."

Francine waved her hands in the air. "Bella won't be here for two weeks. I'll make something special. What's your favorite dinner, Alex?"

"Mac and cheese. Daddy makes the best."

"I'm sure he does, dear." Francine sighed, then skewered Rick with a disapproving stare. "You really must feed her better. I'll make all the arrangements. I'll also talk to Marquetta at the next town council meeting and tell her you need more guidance."

"Please, don't." The problem was, she would. No matter how he felt. He had a business to run in this little town and didn't need the mayor and his cook bickering over how to feed his daughter. "Marquetta has plenty of other duties. We're small, Francine, so we all do everything."

"Tsk, tsk. Once she understands the importance, she'll be happy to help. You're being taken advantage of, Rick. Captain Jack ran a tight ship. His weakness was women, but he employed no slackers."

"He hired Marquetta and sent her to school." Rick didn't mean to, but he crossed his arms and narrowed his gaze at Francine. How could she even think Marquetta didn't pull her weight? Rick's phone chimed. He recognized Marquetta's ringtone. "Excuse me," he said as he backed away, thankful for the interruption. The call had likely prevented him from saying something he'd regret later.

Next to him, Alex clanked her spoon in the dish one last time, then set it on the counter and picked up her small grocery bag. "Thank you Mrs. Carter, your ice cream is the best."

Rick turned away to answer Marquetta's call. "Hey, what's up?"

"Nothing good, I'm afraid."

Marquetta's voice sounded shaky. Very unlike her. Rick hunched forward and whispered. "You sound upset."

"A couple of the guests found Jim Gordon's body down by the bay. You need to get back here right away before they kill each other."

"Wait, wait." Rick glanced over his shoulder. Gordon was dead? Thank goodness Alex was talking to Francine. His daughter wouldn't hear the conversation, but Francine probably would. She was obviously multitasking—eavesdropping with one side of her brain while she chitchatted with the other. That meant any questions he asked now would raise her suspicions. "I can be there in a few minutes, but can you clarify what's going on for me?"

"The guests, Rick. Mr. Kalstone found Mr. Gordon's body on the rocks. Now they're all down there messing with the body and accusing each other of murder."

7

ALEX

My dad looks kinda mad. He's got his scrunchy face on. It sounds like he's talking to Marquetta, but she usually makes him laugh and now he looks real serious. I wanna ask him what's wrong, but Mrs. Carter's bell rings. It's a man and a woman. They look young. And real happy. Like they just got married or something. They're probably from out of town cause Mrs. Carter is acting all sweet to them. She does that with visitors.

"Let's go, Alex. Francine has customers, and our groceries are getting warm." My dad puts away his phone and his jaw puckers.

I look up at him outside Mrs. Carter's shop. "Are you mad at me, Daddy? Did I do something wrong?"

Before he can answer, Deputy Cunningham drives by. He's got the red lights on and his siren makes me want to cover my ears.

"Something bad happened at the B&B. We have to hurry back."

"What, Daddy?" He starts walking, but I stop, not sure I can take another step until I know. Is it Marquetta? I bite my lower lip to hold back the tears. "Is Marquetta okay?"

"She's fine, kiddo." My dad smiles at me. "That was her on the phone. It's Mr. Gordon. He's dead. The guests are all down at the shore."

Mr. Gordon is dead? Wow. That's messed up. We walk faster, but by the time we get to the next corner I've got a plan. This could be really good. It'll let my dad do what makes him happy—investigate.

"Are you gonna help Deputy Cunningham, Daddy?"

"What? No, of course not. Why would you ask that?"

"Cause everybody knows Deputy Cunningham isn't a real cop."

"Let's go." My dad huffs and gives me "the dad" look. "The deputy is a sworn officer."

"He reads water meters! He doesn't know what to do."

"That doesn't make him less official. Besides, who told you such a thing?"

"All the kids at school. Robbie Sachetti says the chief has short-timers and Deputy Cunningham has no-timers."

"We need to get home. And Alex, you and I are having a long talk tonight."

8

RICK

The moment Rick and Alex walked through the front door, Alex looked up and asked, "Daddy, can I see the dead guy?"

"No. Absolutely no way."

She walked away with her shoulders slumped, carrying her grocery bag into the kitchen. Rick followed and placed his bag on the counter next to Alex's as he gazed out the window. Deputy Adam Cunningham was balancing himself on a craggy, moss-covered boulder gesturing for the guests to move away. But each time he turned his back on one person, another slipped behind him.

Rick's jaw fell as he squinted at the scene in the distance. "What are those people doing?"

"They're looking for Mr. Gordon's piece of the map! I can't believe this. Adam is so over his head, Rick. You've got to help him out."

"Good grief." Rick strode out the door to help with crowd control. He crossed the patio to the path which led to the shore. He wasn't even halfway there when the deputy caught his eye and waved frantically. Rick trotted the rest of the distance.

"Hey, you..." Deputy Cunningham yelled at a man who was inching toward the victim.

"That's Cadman Richardson," Rick said. "He's Jim Gordon's former business partner." Rick raised his voice so the others would hear him over the sound of the surf. "All of you need to line up over here by me or Deputy Cunningham will arrest you for tampering with a crime scene. Won't you, Deputy?"

Adam seemed torn. He hesitated for a moment before appearing to make up his mind. "Rick's right," he barked. "This is a crime scene and how the victim died has not been determined. Therefore, anyone going near the victim will be arrested for interfering in a police investigation." He planted his hands on his belt buckle and spread his feet shoulder-width apart. "That applies to you, too, Mr. Richardson."

Finally, thought Rick. Deputy Adam Cunningham actually sounded like a cop. The crime-scene talk was probably all BS. Gordon had most likely slipped, hit his head, and bled to death. However, it never hurt to be cautious, and these idiots needed to show a little respect. "Right. Everybody get over here by me."

Rick waited as his guests glumly filed over one-by-one to stand next to him. Heath Santiago was the last to fall in line. It wasn't the most even row he'd ever seen, but it would do. At least they were no longer contaminating any possible evidence.

"Let me get a few preliminary photos." Rick pulled out his cell phone, instinctively doing what he'd done for years when reporting as R.J. Atwood in New York. He turned on the camera, shot an overview photo of the entire scene, then stopped and eyed the wet corpse.

Face down, sprawled across the rocks, it looked as though he might have died instantly. But, why were the clothes dripping wet? The body couldn't have washed up on those rocks because the tide was low. Besides, Gordon had been alive during high tide this morning.

Rick leaped from one rock to the next until he was about ten feet from his previous position. He took another photo. As he focused on the shot, he noticed a wound on the back of the head. There were only two possible solutions. The first was some weird weather anomaly—Jim Gordon could have fallen into the ocean, drowned, and then a mini-tsunami could have tossed his battered body onto those rocks. Now that was an unlikely scenario. More like, impossible. Which left one other option. This was murder.

He approached slowly, taking more pictures with each step. When he finished, he looked at Adam. "I'll share these, but you may want to take your own, too."

Deputy Cunningham glanced around the scene before pointing to a black nylon bag a short distance away. "I was in such a hurry to get everyone away from the body when I got here that I just dropped it on the sidewalk." He hopscotched the rocks until he reached the sidewalk.

"Everybody stay where you are," Rick snapped when Mr. Richardson stepped out of line. He stared at each one and they all, except for Mr. Santiago, averted their gaze.

He waited while Adam knelt and unpacked his camera bag. The onshore breeze was gusting at about 15-25 mph. Under other circumstances, it would be refreshing. Not here, not now.

When Deputy Cunningham returned, Rick lowered his voice. He did not want the others hearing this conversation. "Where's the chief?"

"Del's off sick and the chief is at some fancy training seminar the mayor sent him to."

Terrific. Alex had been right about the deputy. He split his time between reading water meters, doing the billing, and police work. The poor guy had never handled this kind of investigation. "Have you thought about calling for assistance, Adam? What about bringing in the sheriff? This should be documented properly— what if there was foul play? If you don't do everything by the book, the evidence could be thrown out of court."

Adam winced and glanced at the body. "I don't know."

"At the very least we should be meticulous until a medical professional certifies the cause of death."

"I know, but Mayor Carter doesn't want outside interference."

"Interference? I hardly think help from the sheriff would be seen as—wait, when did she tell you this?"

The deputy blew out a breath as he eyed Gordon's body. "The chief gave me specific instructions to call her if anything big happened, so I did. I called before I left the station. She said you might help out."

"Me? I was a reporter, not a cop." Rick groaned. Mayor Francine Carter ran the town the same way she did Scoops & Scones, on a whim fueled by plenty of gossip. He shouldn't be surprised she wanted him to consult on a murder. "Have you ever conducted an investigation? Of any type?"

"I...um...took a night class after I got hired. The town paid for the class, but Mayor Carter said I shouldn't get too fancy because I might educate myself out of a job."

Rick breathed deeply as he peered at the house. Alex and Marquetta were watching from the kitchen window. He knew what they'd say—help out. "Tell you what, Adam, let's get all of this documented. I can escort them inside and we'll do our best to keep them under control until you're done out here. After that, you can interview as many of them as you want."

He stood back and looked from the guests up to the house. He'd never heard of a single murder happening in Seaside Cove. And now, the impossible had happened, right here at the B&B.

The question was, what would he do about it?

9

RICK

It didn't take long to herd the guests into the dining room. It was Rick's job to stand in the corner and ensure they didn't compare notes about Gordon's death. None of them appeared to be in a talking mood, making the job simple enough. After what he'd seen at breakfast, he wasn't sure anyone in this room liked even one of the others. Miss Potok and Miss Kelley seemed pleasant enough, but Hayden Kalstone—wow—what a piece of work he was. And then there was the confrontation downtown between Cadman and Mr. Gordon. According to Francine, it had almost turned violent, which meant there was no love lost between those two either.

Rick knew little about the other three—Brad Luhan, Heath Santiago, and Mark Joshua—other than they'd also been scouring the area around the body. Did any of these people have a brain? Or were they so focused on that map they'd do anything to find it?

Marquetta brought in water and glasses. She served each guest before leaving quietly. Rick checked the time. Adam was taking longer than he'd expected, but Rick wouldn't let the group go until they'd all given the deputy their statements. As the minutes ticked by, Rick kept picturing Gordon's body—clothes wet as though he'd been in the ocean.

He muttered, "So who found him?"

"Hayden," Monica said.

Rick started at her comment. He hadn't even realized he'd asked the question out loud. Her answer, however, was consistent with what Marquetta had told him on the phone. "Were you alone, Mr. Kalstone?"

"No."

"We were on the patio." Monica swiped away the tears on her cheeks. "Hayden tried to save him. He gave CPR."

"I don't believe that for a second," Heath snarled, then turned on Hayden. "You hated Jim. Why would you want to help him?"

"I didn't hate him," Hayden shot back. "I wondered what drove him. He was a man obsessed."

"You're the man obsessed," Mark glanced at Rick. "Hayden's always pretending to be so dispassionate about things, but he's easily as greedy as the rest of this bunch."

"Oh, and you're not?" Monica snapped before she pinned Reese with a vicious sneer. "And her, she's a lying slut. She raised her skirt for anyone who told her they'd lead her to the San Manuel."

"Get over yourself, Monica." Reese scowled at her. "I did solid research and didn't do it on my back like you."

"That's not what Jim said." Monica snickered as she sat back in her chair with a self-satisfied grin.

"Enough," Rick barked. "I'm sorry I asked. You people are to sit here quietly and not speak at all. Got it?"

The group turned sullen, nodded, and avoided looking at each other. Marquetta appeared in the doorway and gestured for Rick to approach. He went to her, but made sure the others knew he was still watching.

She leaned toward him and whispered. "Adam needs to ask you a question."

Rick glared at the treasure hunters. "Nobody moves or talks. Marquetta will keep an eye on you. The first person to speak will spend the night in jail." As he walked away, Rick wondered if the town even had a jail. He'd never heard of one. Nor did he have any desire to visit.

Deputy Cunningham stood at the edge of the patio, a short distance beyond the Adirondack chairs where Rick encountered Mr. Gordon earlier. The memory sent a chill down Rick's spine. How quickly a man could die. "Hey, Adam. Marquetta said you had a question."

"She told me these treasure hunters all have rooms booked for a couple more days. Is that right?"

"Sure is. Why?"

"I wanted to make sure you can keep them here. I told them they couldn't leave town yet."

"Looks like we'll have to work for our money then." Rick winked at Adam and chuckled. He thought it was kind of funny. After all, he wasn't being paid to help. But Adam apparently didn't see the humor and a few seconds of silence followed.

Finally, the deputy said, "What do I do with the body? I can't... just leave it. The tide's coming in. It'll wash away. The mayor doesn't want me calling for help, and like I said, the chief is out of town, and Del is down with the flu. He's the senior officer, so I'm in a real jam."

Rick gazed down to the shore and sighed. The deputy was right. With the tide on its way in, they had to act quickly or the wave action would wash away any possible evidence. Even the body might be swept out to sea if the tide rose high enough. This was where New York cops had a huge advantage. They dealt with crime scenes all the time. Everybody had an assigned task. Poor Adam was in the worst possible position. There was only one thing Rick could do if he ever wanted to look himself in the eye again.

He took the deputy's shoulder and guided him toward the shore. "You're right, Adam. We need to act fast. Here's what we're going to do."

10

ALEX

Hey Journal,

This really sucks.

I got put in a time out. Marquetta caught me watching Miss Potok and Miss Kelley argue over something. She made me come up to my room. I tried to tell Marquetta that they didn't like each other, but she wouldn't listen. She said this murder thing was grownup business and I shouldn't be spying on the guests.

She also said Daddy might help Deputy Cunningham. After what he said to Mrs. Carter about spending more time with me, I bet he might like it if I help out.

I'm gonna do some investigating on my own. But I don't wanna get caught again so I need a lookout. I'm texting Robbie Sachetti to come over. Everybody's gonna think me and Robbie are just playing, but we're gonna help solve the case. Nobody pays attention to us kids so we'll be, like, invisible. Daddy's gonna be super proud when he finds out. It's gonna be awesome. Just like it was in New York when I helped him write his stories.

Alex

11

RICK

Rick's plan to keep Deputy Cunningham out of hot water with Mayor Carter was simple. He'd have the deputy guard the body while Rick called for an ambulance. Once the medical professionals certified the death, an avalanche of bureaucracy would begin to slide downhill. Even the mayor couldn't stop something that big once it started.

He and the deputy searched the surrounding area for clues to how Jim Gordon died, but they found none. No big shock there as far as Rick was concerned. By the time Deputy Cunningham finished taking statements from each of the guests, there was still nothing definitive. With any luck, an examination of the body would provide something more concrete than "he's dead."

Rick stood at the French doors staring out beyond the back patio. The walls suddenly felt restrictive; he needed fresh air. Alex was in her room and Marquetta finishing preparations for tomorrow's breakfast.

With each of his footsteps on the hardwood floor toward Marquetta, his pulse raced faster. When she glanced up at him, he knew he had to do this before he lost his courage.

"Can we go outside for a few minutes and talk?"

"Let me put these loaves away and I'm done."

With the bread stored for the following day, they went outside and stood silently. Rick let the serene atmosphere soak in. Neither said a word until he nudged her in the side. "You're an amazing cook. Did you learn all that in school?"

"Most of it. Some came from my mom. I'm also sort of a mad scientist. I like experimenting with ingredients. When it works, it's great. When it doesn't, well, not so much."

"You've never produced a bad meal here." Rick caught himself watching her.

"Let's call any experimenting I do on the job tame."

They both laughed. The sound of her laugh made him want to ask his questions even more. He needed to do it while they were on the subject.

"So why did Captain Jack send you to that fancy school in San Francisco?"

Marquetta averted her eyes, and her brow furrowed as she looked at the ground. Something tormented her. Why would she not talk about it? For a moment, he thought she contemplated a dark decision. Was this it?

"That's not something I can discuss." She swallowed hard and winced. "I'm sorry."

His heart broke at the pain she must be feeling. He should reach out, take her hand, tell her he cared.

"Let's call it a day, okay? We both have big days ahead of us tomorrow. You have a murder to solve, and I've got a dozen guests to cook for. I'll see you in the morning."

She did an abrupt about-face and left. It was that quick. He couldn't think of what to say, other than to mutter, "Right, see you then."

He scrutinized the white siding of the B&B—another feature that had been part of the "grand remodel." In some ways, the changes to the exterior symbolized what little he knew of his grandfather's life. He whispered, "What kinds of secrets did you have, Captain Jack?"

His shoulders slumped; he might never know. Besides, he needed to start dinner soon. With a last look out to sea, he headed into the kitchen.

No sooner had he closed the door than Reese appeared. She occupied the same spot where he and Marquetta had been. He glanced at the clock on the wall. Quarter after five. Should he leave her alone?

Reese pulled her thigh-length sweater closer. The sun was still high above the horizon, but one thing he'd learned about Seaside Cove was how quickly the gusting breeze off the ocean chilled the air. What the heck? Everyone reacted to death differently and in her case she might need to talk. He was the innkeeper. Wasn't that like a bartender? He opened the door and stepped out onto the patio.

At the sound created when the door sealed shut, Reese turned, wiped a tear from her cheek, and sniffled. "Have you come to cheer me up?"

Rick shrugged and gave her a consoling smile. "If you need it."

Her watery blue eyes didn't waver from his scrutiny. Her confidence impressed him. It also confused him. Was he attracted to her?

"I've always been controlled by worry," Reese said. "Am I overweight? Will I lose my job?" She choked back a laugh and squinted at Rick. "Do my ears stick out too much?"

"You're far from overweight. You've got a runner's physique. And your ears? They only stick out a little—gives you that sexy pixie look. I can't help with your job, though."

She clutched her arms to her chest. "I get cold easy, too."

The sweater's heavy weave of blacks, grays, and white yarns looked warm enough, yet she still shivered. "Not used to the sea breeze, Miss Potok?"

"Please, call me Reese. I live in San Clemente, so I should be used to it. But, I don't deal well with dampness. It seems worse here."

"Maybe it's stress. It could be affecting your resistance to the cold. It can be terribly draining."

Seagulls rode the air currents above as Reese seemed to ponder the idea. She frowned and turned to face the shoreline. "Jim had a slew of medical problems, not the least of which was his mental state. He was—disturbed. What it comes down to is simple. He was a strange man and didn't have a lot of friends. We were alike in that way; neither of us were fond of the party scene."

"Disturbed? How so?"

"Can we leave it at that?"

"Sure. Did you see much of each other?"

"We were friendly."

"Sounds to me like you're going to miss him. Were you close?"

After a long pause, her jaw tightened. "If you want to be cliché about it, we were strictly casual. We attended a few parties together, but for Jim and me it was some sort of weird addiction. We couldn't focus on fun when we had so much work to do. That's what really bound us—finding the *San Manuel*, getting the job done."

In a way, the relationship she described reminded Rick of his connection with Marquetta. Bound by duty? Or pulled apart by it?

The breeze whispered overhead through the clump of fir trees at the edge of the patio. A distinct chill filled the air. Clouds hung low on the horizon. California coastal living, thought Rick. The day was drawing to a close, and he still had questions about what he'd seen that morning. There was the encounter between Monica and Jim Gordon. At the time, he'd wondered if they were lovers, or if the relationship was one-sided. Unrequited love? He cleared his throat. "I hope you don't mind if I ask a personal question, but I thought Monica was involved with Mr. Gordon."

She brushed away a few strands of blonde-streaked hair blown across her face by a gust of wind. Her blue eyes once again brimmed with moisture. "No. Monica wanted to be with Jim, but he wanted nothing to do with her. She's a let's-settle-down kind of girl—her goal in life is to get married, have a passel of kids, and attend PTA meetings. Jim and I both had too many other things to do, you know? If Mr. Right comes along, that's great. But I won't daydream my life away."

"I understand completely. It's been a while since I've had time to daydream."

"I'll bet. You have a daughter and a business to run. You're not married?"

How did he answer that? Could he? "I suppose I'm a cliché, too. It's complicated."

She laughed and nodded. "The story of our lives."

"I get it," he said as he gazed at the horizon, then massaged the spot behind his right ear where the tension had been building all day. He inclined his head from side-to-side.

"Headache?"

"Long day, I guess." Had she been watching him? He leaned back on his heels and held her gaze. "You must have those, too. Researching sunken treasure ships—that has to be tedious."

She shivered, then glanced over her shoulder at the house. "At times."

"I'm fascinated. This morning, you said you'd researched the *San Manuel*. How extensive was it?"

"Enough to know there's a problem with the legend."

Rick's stomach fluttered. The legend? He'd told it to Francine almost as a ruse, but deep down he'd hoped it was real. "What kind of problem?"

"There are no solid facts one way or the other, but by the 1560s, the cargo on those galleons was incredibly valuable. The silver and gold from the New World supported Spain's economy and privateers from other countries made the voyages very dangerous. So, I keep asking myself, why did the *San Manuel* sail off on its own?"

The fluttering increased, and Rick had an urge to do what he'd done as a reporter—raise more questions and dig for confirmation with a second source. "Did you collaborate with Mr. Gordon on your research?"

"Jim wasn't much of a collaborator."

"Then why'd he set up this weekend?"

"I'm not sure." She forced a smile. "I need to go in. Is there someplace in town that's good for dinner?"

"Try the Crooked Mast. It's a funny name but they've been around forever and the food is amazing. The place is a favorite of all the locals."

"Thanks."

Some emotion Rick couldn't read played out on her face over the next few seconds as she looked at him. He was about to offer the classic penny for her thoughts when she bobbed her head and walked away.

Rick stared after her. Had he just been asked on a date? That wasn't happening. He had Alex to think of and had a nagging desire to walk the shoreline one more time. Perhaps in a different light—and with the shock of finding a body behind him—he'd see things more clearly.

He passed between the fir trees and followed the path to the shore. The tide was coming in and would soon make traversing the rocks treacherous. The roar of heavy surf drowned out all other sounds. White foamy spray tingled his skin and left the moss-covered surface slick with spray. He tasted the salt on his lips. So enchanting. So dangerous.

But, it was tempting. What if he moved slowly? A series of swells rolled in. Rick counted the seconds between each. No, there wasn't enough time between them to avoid being drenched or knocked over.

Another heavy surge exploded directly in front of him. A plume of spray rose ten feet into the air and dissipated as it drifted past. He breathed in the heavy, wet air and sighed as he scrutinized the crime scene. He hated to admit it, but the B&B now had one of those. It was time to make Alex's dinner, but later tonight he would go through his photos from this afternoon.

He turned away from the questions dominating his thoughts, gazed up at the B&B, and saw Reese standing outside the dining

47

room French doors. He quickened his step, and she retreated into the house. Another mystery to unravel? Perhaps, because he did feel an urge to discover what secrets she might be guarding.

12

RICK

Rick and Alex sat side-by-side at the end of the center island. White granite, marbled with gray veins stretched before them. Glossy white cabinets, several with glass panes, rose to the ceiling. This was a far cry from the small apartment they'd had in New York.

"Daddy?"

"What, kiddo?"

"I like Marquetta's oven stew. A lot." Alex sopped up some of the broth with the French bread they'd purchased at Crusty Buns.

Rick broke off a piece from his own slice and did the same. "Your taste buds must be changing. You never used to be much for stews." He looked again at her plate. "Wow, clean as a whistle. You know, we had tons of bakeries in our old neighborhood, but Crusty Buns is as good as any of those."

"Daddy..."

"Okay. I won't make a big deal of it. You're growing up. Just don't run off and get married. Your old man couldn't take the strain of losing his daughter so soon." He leaned over, kissed her forehead, and winked.

She rolled her eyes and wrinkled her nose. "Okay."

After dinner, they hung out in Rick's room and watched TV until Alex's bedtime. He sent her off to brush her teeth and put her jammies on. When he entered her room to tuck her in, she held out the hairbrush.

His vision misted over; his throat tightened. Was she asking him to do what he'd done when she was little? Gladly. When he finished, he handed the hairbrush to Alex. She kissed him on the cheek and gave him a hug. "Thanks, Daddy."

She climbed into bed and he helped fluff up her pillow. When that was done, he straightened the coverlet.

"Daddy..."

"I'm fawning, aren't I?"

"It's okay." She smiled up at him. "It's kinda nice sometimes. But don't get used to it. You can't do it all the time."

"Right. At least I've got now." Though exhaustion weighed him down like a yoke around his neck, he did not want their few minutes to end. These were the moments he looked forward to all day. This little snippet of time was the one he cherished most. The two of them could talk without interruption or distraction. Connect. If only for a few precious minutes. "Today's been stressful for everyone," he said. "I can't imagine how bad it must have been for you."

"It's not your fault, Daddy. Are you gonna find out who killed Mr. Gordon?"

What did he say to that? His daughter was precocious and fearless, and he often lay awake at night wondering how to keep her safe from a world spiraling out of control. He opted for noncommittal. "Deputy Cunningham is in charge of the investigation."

"No way. He needs your help."

"I'll consider it."

"Is that what you told Marquetta? She said you'd help."

He reached up and made an adjustment to the covers. "That's not exactly what I said. I told her I'd think about it."

"Oh."

Alex scooted up against the pillow and she sat straighter. She had her mom's freckles, red-flecked hair, and blue eyes. Every time she smiled, he saw Giselle in her. The girl-next-door he'd married, not the star-struck career seeker.

"What's wrong, Daddy? You look sad."

He shook his head and steadied himself with a deep breath. Only recently had he come to accept that Giselle was their past, Seaside Cove, their future. He glanced around. White, antiqued furniture—a small desk, dresser, and a headboard—all matched thanks to Marquetta's help. The aqua and purple color scheme gave Alex's room a classic, girly appearance.

"You and Marquetta did a nice job in here."

"I love it. It's all my favorite colors."

"You like Marquetta, don't you, Alex?"

"She's the best."

"Well, I like her, too. But, men and women don't have to be... involved. They can be just friends."

"Like you and Marquetta?"

"Exactly." Rick nodded, not sure what words to use next. Stick to the message, he told himself. No more matchmaking. He smoothed the purple backing on the coverlet and bit his lower lip. "Alex, you remember what happened at Scoops & Scones today?"

"You mean getting ice cream from Mrs. Carter?" Her brow furrowed, and she shrugged. "Sure."

"The ice cream was a good idea. I really like it, too. Going there made me realize something. It's about Bella."

Alex's face lit up. "We're gonna go to Mrs. Carter's for dinner?"

"No," he said quietly, but firmly. "That's what we need to talk about."

The smile disappeared. Apparently, she already understood what was coming. He didn't want to belabor the point, but he did need her to understand how he felt. "Alex, ever since your mom and I separated I've been trying to figure out my life. But, those are decisions I have to make on my own. Bella Carter is way too young for me and you should not be attempting to play matchmaker for me. Do you understand?"

"Yes, Daddy. I'm sorry."

"Good girl." He got up and stood at the door with his fingers resting on the wall switch. He waited. Watched. And realized how lucky he was to have her. "Goodnight, kiddo."

"G'night, Daddy."

He flipped off the light and closed the door behind him. Not until he was standing in the hallway did he realize Alex had only said she understood. She hadn't promised to not do it again. He sighed. Bella might be off the list, but that left a whole bunch of mothers in this town with daughters they'd like to marry off.

Rick shuffled down the hall to his office and entered what he considered his sanctuary from chaos. He let his attention flit from one part of the room to another. The atmosphere surrounded him. Brought him solace. Whenever he was here, it was as though he'd been transported back in time. Captain Jack had loved the mahogany desk, leather chair, and floor-to-ceiling bookshelves. The smell of leather and old books clung like moss to everything.

At his computer, Rick examined the photos he'd taken of the body and the surrounding area. Twenty-one altogether. That included several tight shots from varying distances and angles.

A low moan pierced the air. Rick glanced at the window. As usual, he'd left it open a crack. The noise was nothing more than the breeze whistling through the opening. He slid the paned glass up and drank in the moisture. The temperature hung in the mid sixties and the distant crash of waves created a steady peaceful thrum.

Rick returned to his computer and continued scrolling through photos. One-by-one, he zoomed in and scrutinized what the camera captured. At ten-thirty he sat back, no longer able to fend off the exhaustion overtaking him. How ridiculous was this? He was going cross-eyed examining all this detail. For what? He'd found nothing.

He closed up the office and headed downstairs for some water. Tomorrow he might spend more time looking through the photos. But to what end? He didn't bother turning on a light. Instead, he navigated around the kitchen island by moonlight. He pulled a glass from the cabinet, filled it, and stood in the darkness to gaze out the window.

Silver moonbeams glinted off the waves. A never-ending parade of iridescent white streamers marched toward shore. His shoulders ached from too much time spent leaning over the screen of his laptop. He opened the patio door and went outside.

With his eyes closed, Rick listened to the sounds of the sea. Distant surf. A steady rhythm so calming it quieted his soul. Even the ocean air brought a fresh and new feeling to everything. Seaside Cove had captured his heart. He hoped Alex felt the same. Did she want to leave? He didn't—and he needed to face reality. "File the divorce papers," he muttered. "Put Giselle behind you."

He rolled his shoulders while gazing at the bay. A glint of light caught his attention. He blinked and stared more closely. Was that a flashlight down by the rocks? His mind had to be playing tricks on him.

The longer he watched, the more obvious it became. This was no illusion. Someone was wandering around on the shore. Only the surefooted or the foolhardy ventured out there at night. In the daytime, the area was tricky—as they'd seen earlier. But now? The conditions were nothing less than treacherous.

Who would be stupid enough to go out there? It had to be one of those treasure hunters. What if it was Reese? Had she been planning her return when he'd talked to her earlier? One wrong step and she'd crack her head open. The thought sent a chill down the length of his spine.

Rick set his glass on the patio table. He rushed to the kitchen and grabbed the flashlight. He kept the beam off as he followed the path to the shore. The last thing he needed was for that idiot out there to panic when they saw him coming. Whether it was Reese or one of the others he was obligated to warn them about the dangers. After that, if they stayed, it was at their own risk.

He was at shore level when the flashlight holder, a silhouette in the white glow of the moon, stooped down. Rick stopped in his tracks. That was not Reese. She was much smaller. This was a man. And what had he picked up? A weapon? What if this was Gordon's killer? Oh my God, he might be the one in danger.

Rick reached for his phone, but didn't pull it from its holster. Adam wouldn't be happy about a false alarm. He sucked in a breath and shot an involuntary glance over his shoulder at the B&B. Alex's bedroom light shined behind the white curtains. Why was she still up? He'd have to go check on her later, right after he dealt with this midnight stranger. Rick took a step forward and flicked on the high-powered beam.

13

RICK

"Mr. Richardson, what are you doing out here?" Rick yelled. The moon slipped behind a passing cloud, casting a shadow over them. "It's dangerous out on those rocks. Especially at night. And what's that you're holding?"

It was as though fear—or guilt—had frozen the man in place. His horn-rimmed glasses reflected the beam from Rick's torch and his arms hung at his sides. In his left hand he held a long black cylinder about the size of a one-inch pipe. Cadman glanced down before turning back toward the bay. He raised his hand a few inches as a large breaker crashed immediately before him.

A wall of spray rode in on the breeze and Rick squinted through the mist. Was Cadman going to throw the object into the bay? "Stop! They'll find it. This town has more divers than you can count. Get over here."

A drizzle of mist settled around the man as he stared back at Rick. He sighed and took a step, but his foot slipped and he tottered for a second. He recovered his balance and hopscotched across the rocks until he stood on the paved walkway next to Rick.

"It's my monopod. You know, a one-legged camera tripod. I laid it down when I was taking some sunset shots." He shielded his eyes against the intense beam and cocked his head to the side. "Just forgot about it. No big deal, huh?"

"Sunset photos?" What a crock. "Those are my favorites," Rick lied. "Can I see them?"

"Well, none of them turned out. I...deleted them."

"Come with me. You have some explaining to do."

Rick lowered the beam to Cadman's chest and pointed it at the man's back as they returned to the B&B. They entered through the kitchen and the moment he stepped inside, Rick realized how much bite the breeze coming off the bay held. He kept Cadman in front of him as they made their way to the dining room. Rick flipped on the light switch and squinted against the sudden glare.

"Nothing like going from dark to brilliant daylight to blind you, huh?" Cadman's laugh sounded forced.

Rick indicated the four-seater table between them with the beam of the flashlight. "Put that thing down."

"Okay, okay. Let's not go crazy." Cadman placed the monopod on the table, then buried his face in his hands. "I know how this looks, but it's all perfectly innocent."

Rick wasn't so sure. He turned off the flashlight, but cradled it in his right hand just in case he needed some sort of weapon. Cadman had on a tan jacket with a blue-striped hood layered around the collar. Beneath his jacket, he wore a checkered flannel shirt and beneath that, a T-shirt. "You're dressed like someone planning to spend a long night in the cold. I think there's more to it than what you're saying. Before he died, Jim Gordon and I were talking. He told me you broke up the business partnership. He said it cost the company a lot of money. Do you want to tell me your side of the story?"

Cadman stroked his chin and neck. He shook his head and smiled to himself before he spoke. "Figures he'd spin things so he'd look better. The truth puts me in first place for the 'I Hate Jim Gordon Club.' But you have to understand, everybody else here despised him as much as I did."

"All I want is for you to tell me what happened." It was approaching midnight, long past the time Rick wanted to let this guy dish on the others. The critical question was should he wake up Deputy Cunningham or not?

"It's true, we were in business, but we never formed a legal partnership. And I'm not the one who ended things. He was. Well, technically, I did walk away, but he forced me out by plagiarizing my designs. He even had the audacity to take credit for my work with Nike. Everything I'd done, he sold under his name. The man committed fraud."

"How so?"

"Jim and I worked on contract with Nike. We were a couple of kids playing with shoes and making tons of money at the same time. Everything blew up when I left on my honeymoon. I met my wife in June of last year. We were married after a whirlwind romance. Jim was even the best man at my wedding. Nancy and I booked a two-week cruise to get away. The timing wasn't good because of a big deal in the works for a new design I'd come up with. It was revolutionary—that's what it was."

"So everything was going your way. You were living the good life. You had a new idea, a new wife, and were taking off on a romantic honeymoon. What was wrong with that?"

"While I was sailing the ocean blue, Jim took my idea to Nike and sold it as his. He left me out of the negotiations. Never told Nike about me. When I returned, Jim informed me there was a new contract with them and I was now working for him. We had a big knock-down-drag-out fight. I got so mad I was going to sue. To make a long story short, my attorney said it would be easier to settle for a payout than attempt to prove fraud. We were dealing with intellectual property rights, and I had not signed the designs—which Jim had done in my absence."

"Okay, so you hated him. Does that mean you committed murder?"

"Not a chance." Cadman emitted a nervous laugh. "Since that day, I've envisioned myself bashing him on the head with a blunt instrument over and over until he admitted what he'd done. Or died. You could say when he stole my design and claimed it for his own, he also took my soul. I've been cold inside thinking about his betrayal. On top of it all, my wife and I are separated. She says I'm no longer the man she married. Of course I'm not. Jim Gordon drove a knife into that man's back. I would have loved to return the favor."

"Sounds like a solid motive."

"Told you."

"So you did." Rick pointed at the black tube. It was about two feet long and an inch in diameter. Midway between a golf club and a baseball bat. Definitely sturdy enough to crush a man's skull. "Is that the murder weapon?"

"I don't know, but the truth is, I wanted that scum alive more than anyone else. He took everything from me, but I finally had what I needed for my case. I fired the incompetent jerk who called himself an attorney and got myself one with some smarts. You can call him. I'll let him know it's okay. With Jim alive, I stood a chance to recover the money I'd lost. With him dead I'm back to the beginning. How am I supposed to sue a dead man? What I really wanted was to have him suffer the humiliation of losing in court. His pain would have lasted a lifetime. Now, it's over. The reality is I'm the last one who wanted him dead."

"There are witnesses to the argument you two had this morning. The town mayor says she had to call the police to prevent a fistfight."

Cadman laughed and plopped down into the chair next to him. "Yeah, we got into it. But there's no way I could have fought him or anyone else. Whether I wanted to or not."

Rick eyed Cadman while he waited for an answer. When it wasn't forthcoming, he asked, "Why?"

The man raised his right arm until it was just below the height of his shoulder. At that point he winced and dropped it to his side. "I'm a swimmer, but I have a torn rotator cuff. Every time I push too hard, I get this excruciating pain right here." He touched a spot on his shoulder, pressed it, and winced again. "A few months ago, right after my wife left, I was under so much stress I really threw myself back into my swimming workouts. I swam no matter how bad it got. By the time I broke down and went to the doctor, I'd messed it up good. I'll have him release the report if you want. Fact of the matter is I can't change a lightbulb if it's above my head. And I couldn't throw a punch if my life depended on it. So what are you going to do? Call the cops?"

"Your monopod will have to be tested."

"Go ahead. Doesn't matter to me. I didn't kill him."

"Your prints will be on it. Your DNA, too."

Cadman glanced at the monopod and shrugged. "It is mine."

Rick pulled out his phone to take a photo of the supposed weapon. While he was framing his shot, he asked, "So if you didn't kill Gordon, how did you know this was down there?"

"A little birdie told me."

"I'm in no mood for coy, Mr. Richardson."

"All right," Cadman huffed. "Let's just say I remembered where I left it."

Enough of this BS. Rick snapped the photo, then placed the call to Deputy Cunningham. He kept the phone to his ear as the line rang. "You're not giving me much choice," he grumbled.

A few seconds later, a groggy voice answered. It sounded as though Adam had been dragged out of a sound sleep. "Rick? Is that you? What time is it?"

"Sorry, Deputy, but this is official business. You need to come over here. We have a new development in the investigation. Cadman Richardson just turned up something very suspicious."

14

ALEX

June 16

Hey Journal,

I can't sleep. I keep thinking about Mr. Gordon. Did somebody kill him because he wasn't a nice man?

I was looking out my window when Daddy came in with Mr. Richardson. I snuck downstairs to listen and heard them talking about Mr. Richardson being the killer. It's not him, Journal. It can't be cause he's got a bad shoulder. He told my dad that, but I don't think Daddy believes him. Besides, I know who the killer is. It's that Miss Potok. She acts all nice with my dad, but she's really not.

Deputy Cunningham almost saw me when he got here. I would've been totally busted. Later, they put Mr. Richardson in Deputy Cunningham's car. He's gonna get arrested and it's totally unfair cause he couldn't have done it.

Daddy and Deputy Cunningham are kinda stuck. They said they can't get a warrant to find any clues. That's gotta be why Daddy was so mad about me trying to get us invited to dinner with Mrs. Carter. It's not a good time for distractions.

Daddy said he doesn't want me to worry about him, but I do. Without my mom, we gotta look out for each other. Maybe Marquetta will know who else would be good for my dad.

Tomorrow, I'm gonna help solve Mr. Gordon's murder. It's gonna be super tense around here cause nobody's telling the truth. That's why everybody's so jumpy. They're all hiding something.

I'm gonna text Robbie. We can do what the cops can't and check out the rooms tomorrow while everybody's at breakfast.

Wish me luck!

Alex

It's really quiet outside again now that Deputy Cunningham left. I hope my dad didn't see my light on when he was bringing in Mr. Richardson, but just in case, I'm hiding under the covers to text Robbie.

—hey Robbie, u up?
—now - doh
—wanna help me
—what do u need
—doing spy work and need a lookout
—cool
—Be here @8
—k gotta go hear my mom coming
—nite
—nite

15

RICK

Rick was dead tired. It was the middle of the night and the few minutes it had taken Deputy Cunningham to arrive at the B&B seemed like hours. The subsequent question-and-answer session dragged on like an endurance test even though it only lasted about twenty minutes.

The deputy took in Cadman's monopod as evidence even though they really had nothing of any substance. Rick trudged upstairs thinking how predictable the end result had been. Cadman wasn't under arrest, but the deputy had taken him in to give a new statement. The unspoken subtext? A pipe dream that Richardson would give in and confess. Not happening, thought Rick.

All he wanted to do now was check on Alex. There was no way for her to deny being up while he'd been outside with that stupid treasure hunter. Her light had been on and he'd seen it in the window. Rick opened the door and peeked in. Moonlight on the curtains cast a diffused white glow over the bed and carpet.

Alex lay on her side, rumpled covers over her but pushed slightly to one side. He slipped into the room, intending to pull down the shade and straighten the covers. As he stood by the bed,

Rick looked over at Alex's desk. Her phone wasn't in the charger. He closed his eyes and listened to the murmur of her breath. After a few seconds, he smiled and opened his eyes. "You're awake, aren't you, kiddo?"

She rolled onto her back and looked up at him. "Daddy, how'd you know?"

"I saw your light earlier." And her breathing hadn't been nearly soft enough. Rick straightened the coverlet and sat on the edge of the bed, then stroked her hair. Her eyes sparkled in the dim light and his heart ached. What a tough day for a little girl. "Phone."

She huffed and pulled it from under the covers. "Not fair."

"You don't need to sleep with it. What's up?" There was definitely something going on with her. He could always tell when she had some sort of question. Of course, at ten years old, he shouldn't be surprised.

"Is it normal to be jealous?"

Where had that come from? It definitely wasn't the subject he'd expected. "Are you worried about Mr. Gordon?"

"Yeah. I don't understand why someone killed him. Do you think somebody got jealous? Jealousy sucks."

Even in the semi-darkness Rick could see her lower lip puckered into a pout.

"Are you jealous of someone, Alex?"

"Not me. Robbie Sacchetti."

"Robbie? Isn't he your best friend?"

"He is, but sometimes he gets jealous of the other kids. His dad's been out of work since we got here."

"That's a long time to be without a job. When I graduated from college, I worked for a bank and saw a lot of people lose their homes. Did you ever consider that Robbie might not be jealous as much as he's opening up with you?"

"I guess." Alex shrugged.

The sadness in Alex's voice weighed heavy on Rick's conscience. "We've been lucky, kiddo, you and I. More than many others. In New York, I knew reporters who were always angry because somebody else wrote a better story. They blamed it on everything else except the most important factor of all, themselves. In Robbie's case, his family has gotten some bad breaks. They're holding up as best they can."

Alex scooched up a little straighter and sounded hopeful. "Could we do something to help them?"

"It's possible. We can talk about it tomorrow. Right now, you need to get some shut-eye."

"Okay, but I still don't get why somebody killed Mr. Gordon."

"Neither do I, Alex. Murder never makes sense. I'm sorry you have to go through this."

"It's not your fault, Daddy. Maybe somebody was angry with Mr. Gordon."

"It's possible, kiddo. Whatever the reason, I want to keep you away from these people as much as possible."

"No!" Alex glanced toward her desk, then wrapped her arms around his neck. "Please, Daddy, don't make me go. I like it here."

He hugged Alex in response, then eased her back onto her pillow. When he looked into her moist eyes, he realized how she'd interpreted his words. "I'm not sending you anywhere, kiddo. But, I am going to talk to Marquetta in the morning. One of us needs to be with you at all times until this murder is solved."

There was a long pause as Alex seemed to consider what he'd said. He hated the idea of restricting her movements, but until the guests left or he and Adam solved the murder, it was the only solution that made Rick comfortable. He swallowed hard against a newfound fear. Was raising a child in a B&B really a good idea? All these strangers? People he didn't know coming and going constantly?

There was a bit of a pause, then Alex's face lit up in the moonlight. "Can I stay up here during breakfast? It'd be like camping out."

The self-doubts eased and a little surge of relief rushed through Rick. If Alex was in her room and the guests were downstairs, he wouldn't have to worry about her for at least an hour. He smoothed the soft cotton of the coverlet before making his decision.

"That would be perfect, kiddo." He leaned forward and kissed her forehead. "I love you."

"Me, too, Daddy. Can Robbie come over for breakfast? We won't be any bother."

"Sure, why not? That's a great idea. You can call him first thing tomorrow."

"I did—I mean, we were texting about it."

"Oh, okay. Sounds like you two already have something set up. You sleep tight."

16

RICK

Rick came downstairs at 5:30 AM. The backs of his eyelids felt like sandpaper, his brain, nothing more than a mass of gray mush. He'd barely slept. Visions of Cadman Richardson's guilt-filled face seemed to be everywhere, reminding Rick of how he'd caught Cadman red-handed in the process of retrieving the monopod. He had to be linked to Gordon's murder.

The aroma of brewing coffee greeted Rick at the base of the stairs. Of course, Marquetta was already here. Thank goodness, because multiple doses of caffeine were the only way he'd get through this day. He shuffled toward the kitchen, blinking away the dogged urge to crawl back under the covers rather than face another human being—especially these treasure hunters.

"Wow. You look like you were up half the night. You must have had a rough one." Marquetta crossed to the coffeemaker and poured a fresh mug. "Here. This should help. You feel like talking about it?"

Rick groaned. "Cadman Richardson. My turn for the you-won't-believe-this story." He gave a brief description of the midnight encounter in between gulps of hot, steaming coffee.

"You are correct, that's a hard one to believe. Maybe you need more sleep. Your eyes don't have their usual sparkle."

He snickered. "I'm lucky they're not glued shut. The other half of it has to do with Alex. Her light was on. I saw it from the shore, so I stopped in to see her."

"Is she doing okay? She's probably bothered by Mr. Gordon's death, right?"

"More like worried I'm becoming an old—what's the male equivalent of an old maid?"

"There isn't one. The older men get, the more they're considered a catch. Women, on the other hand—let's say we degenerate into something to avoid."

"That's not true, there are plenty of beautiful older women."

"Men become more distinguished with age. Women just get old."

The corner of her lip curled as though she were holding back a smile. She shrugged, nodded at his mug and said, "Stop feeling sorry for yourself and drink up. Did you get Alex convinced you don't need romance advice from a ten-year-old?"

Rick drank down the last of his first cup. "I wish. I assume I only deferred the inevitable." He pushed his empty mug across the island toward Marquetta. His legs were heavy as stone. "Refill, please. I'm definitely going to need a few more cups to kick my brain into gear."

"What you should have is green tea." She turned, opened the pantry, and pulled out a box with Japanese writing on the side. "It tastes good and it's healthy, too. Antioxidants, Rick. They're much healthier than whiskey." She handed him the box.

Who'd said anything about whiskey? "Tea? Yuck." He set the box down and pushed it away. "I'll stick to coffee this morning. And for your information, I was never a big drinker. I had to work nights. Speaking of work, I need to keep Alex away from this investigation. I'd like one of us to be with her at all times."

Marquetta chuckled. "That should keep her from interfering."

"Do you really believe she would?"

"Seriously?" She raised an eyebrow and cocked her head at him. "Have you met your daughter?"

Rick's cheeks flushed hot. Of course Alex would want to investigate. "You're right."

"I can keep her busy. She's a hard worker and a quick learner." Marquetta pulled eggs, milk, and butter from the refrigerator and set them on the counter. "Kind of reminds me of myself at her age."

"I'll bet you've always been a good worker. You're the best one I've got."

She rolled her eyes, gave him a mock glare, then smiled. "I'm the only one you've got. I think you're lying about something. You weren't a crime reporter in New York, were you? That's only a cover for a much darker life."

"No, that was my wife."

"You are still married."

"In the eyes of the law. I'm not so sure she sees it that way. And it doesn't seem to matter in this town. Why is everyone, including my daughter, trying to get me married off?"

Marquetta pursed her lips. Obviously, she was struggling not to laugh.

"Help me, would you?"

She set down her mug and smiled as she shook her head. "You really don't know, do you?"

"If only I did. Alex blindsided me yesterday. She wanted Francine's ice cream much less than a dinner invitation. What's up with that?"

"Oh, my God. You poor, poor man. You, boss, are the most eligible bachelor in town."

Rick swallowed hard to keep from spitting out his coffee. He got the mouthful down, then began coughing so hard it brought tears to his eyes. When he recovered his voice, he almost choked on his words. "You can't be serious. I'm a catch? If I'm the best they've got, this town is in big trouble. I've got a mountain of debt thanks to my grandfather, I'm still learning a business from the ground up, and my precocious daughter is something between Nancy Drew and...and a marriage broker."

Marquetta's eyes twinkled as she smiled at him. "You are so clueless. Sit down while I explain the Seaside Cove version of the birds and the bees."

Rick took the barstool at the end of the center island. He glanced to his left out the west-facing window. Tinges of pink spanned the horizon. Sunrise was in full swing to the east, but the colors ran across the entire sky like party streamers. "Great sunrise."

"Focus, boss."

He looked back at Marquetta. "Right. So why am I the best hope this town has?"

"There are twenty-two mothers here with daughters they want to marry off. There's a lot of competition. That breeds backbiting and jealousy."

"You're kidding me, right?" Rick watched Marquetta's face, but saw not even the hint of a smile. "Wait, how do you know there are twenty-two?"

"It's a small town. It's not a big number. Pay attention. There are the Planners, the Doers, and the Desperate. It probably works the same for our little band of treasure hunters."

Rick glanced down, carefully sipped more coffee, then raised his hand like a schoolboy needing the restroom. "Can we deal with one set of social dynamics at a time? What's a Planner?"

"Daughters in their teens." Marquetta sighed. "Or younger. We've got three."

"Younger? You mean, like Alex's age?"

Marquetta nodded and went on to explain there were six Doers—those who were "ready to fly on their own."

"So Francine is a Doer," Rick said.

"Check. And a fierce competitor."

Rick massaged his temples to relieve his growing unease. Why had he not heard any of this before? "Let me guess, the Desperate are somewhere near menopause."

"Now you're understanding the marriage process in Seaside Cove. And maybe you have an idea why all those married women were so happy to meet you when you first arrived."

He groaned and stared at her. She had her elbows on the countertop and rested her chin on her hands as she gazed at him with a wicked grin.

"Motherly Love in Seaside Cove is unconstrained by distance or time. The marriage competition starts early and continues until one of the parties is in the grave."

They sat in silence. Coffee. It wasn't nearly enough to deal with this "marriage process." He sucked in a deep breath, gazed out the window for a moment, then turned his attention back to Marquetta. "I'm dead meat, aren't I?"

Her playful eyes held his. "Not if you're nimble." She giggled again. "Just don't drop your guard."

"How about it then? You want to get married?" Rick grinned at her, but his smile fell as he watched her playfulness dissipate and her gaze turn cold.

"I will not be a desperation move."

"I'm...I'm sorry," he stammered. It had just been a joke—and obviously, a bad one. "I didn't mean to offend you."

She cradled her mug in her hands as she watched him. "Apology accepted. Let's talk about something else."

"Right. You mentioned the treasure hunters. Are you saying you think they fall into these groupings?" He waved a hand nonchalantly. "Planners and whatever?"

"Why not? Mr. Gordon was a Planner. Miss Kelley is definitely a Doer from what I hear."

"Hmmm, she may not have been doing as much with Gordon as she let on. Reese told me it was a one-sided relationship."

"Reese?" Marquetta straightened up and glared at him. "Not Miss Potok? You two must be getting cozy."

How did he answer that? Jeez, this conversation had turned into a minefield.

17

RICK

An awkward silence fell between Rick and Marquetta as they slipped into the routine of preparing breakfast. By quarter to seven, Rick's mood had soured. This had never happened since they'd met. Things had always been so easy between the two of them. Why had someone committed murder at his B&B? Was it the murder that was causing so much tension? No, it was that stupid question.

"I'm sorry if I made you uncomfortable," he said. "It was..."

"Shush." Marquetta straightened up, smiled.

Forced. Her exterior was forced. And followed by more silence.

She turned away and walked to the refrigerator where she opened the door and poked her head inside. She spoke as she rummaged around. "Not another word about it. The window washer is coming today. I'll have him do the interior glass in the common areas." She closed the stainless steel door and turned to Rick. "We should probably wait on the guest rooms. I can get those done between bookings."

"Sounds good to me," Rick said halfheartedly. He pretended to inspect the bank of five paned windows lining the wall over the sink. "Just keeping all the glass clean in a place like this is almost a full-time job."

"You're right about that. They do brighten the rooms though."

This was ridiculous. Now they could only talk about business or meaningless drivel?

"What else is going on?" Marquetta asked. "Are you looking into the murder? Or are you only playing midnight monitor for Adam?"

At last. Something with at least a modicum of substance. "How long have you known him?"

"I've known Adam since kindergarten." She paused, then added, "He put bubblegum in my hair once."

"Ouch."

"His mother gave him quite a paddling for that one. Anyway, he'll always be that little boy who sat behind me in class."

"This town has a lot of history."

"You have no idea."

Good. Her smile was genuine. More like...normal. "In a way, all this town dynamics stuff reminds me of what was happening between Gordon and Richardson. I'm not sure I buy the story about Cadman preferring to see Gordon alive. I might want to look into it."

"Serious? Does this mean you're going to help Adam? What brought this on?"

"Several things converging. But, the main one is Alex. She asked me if someone killed Gordon because they were jealous. It is one possible motive." Rick rubbed the back of his neck to loosen the tightness. "But after seeing the way Deputy Cunningham dealt with Cadman last night, I'm convinced he won't solve this without some help. He barely asked any questions."

"He hasn't had much training."

"Doesn't sound like he's had any."

"You said it, not me. Tell you what. You help Adam crack this case and I'll have a little girl talk with Alex. We can discuss boys and how they can be a little dense."

Rick snorted and watched her face. Had that been a dig at him? "Am I one of the dense ones?"

"There are twenty-two mothers who have you in their sights, boss."

"Make that twenty-one. I may have given Francine something bigger than marriage to think about."

"Like?"

"Alex and I were in the shop."

Marquetta nodded. "You felt trapped."

"Like a crab in a pot. Isn't that what you coastal people say?"

She stared at him. "No. We don't."

"Oh. Anyway, I couldn't just rush out, so I told her about the *San Manuel.*"

"Tell me you didn't." Marquetta rolled her eyes.

"What?" Rick asked.

"Nothing."

"What? Tell me. I'm one of the dense ones. Remember?"

Marquetta snickered. "Okay, do you know how many times people have come to this town looking for buried or sunken treasure? I've been living with these stories for as long as I can remember." She picked up her mug and gripped it with both hands. Her eyes were moist and rimmed in red. "My father was always chasing treasure."

"I didn't know," Rick said. "I'm sorry."

"You couldn't have known. I don't...like to talk about it. It's not your fault and I shouldn't have snapped at you." Her voice softened. "Now, I have to work on breakfast while you get water and coffee out to the guests. After that, you're free to go play detective." Marquetta's eyes flicked past Rick, and she raised her mug. "Correction. You're free right after you talk to Devon."

Rick turned, saw his handyman, and did his best to sound cheerful. "Well, Mr. Van Horn, what's up?"

"Hey, Rick. I'm here about that estimate you wanted for fixing the back stairs. I finished all the paperwork last night and thought we could go over it now."

Rick glanced at the clock. Was he supposed to believe Devon made a special trip to discuss business at seven in the morning? Right. Unless Rick had gotten a promotion to the master of the universe, something was up. What did his handyman really want?

18

ALEX

Me and Robbie are starting Phase One of the plan to help my dad. We're at the bottom of the stairs listening to all the guests. They're waiting for breakfast and being super mean to each other. They keep arguing about Mr. Gordon's murder. That's awesome cause it means they're gonna be at the table awhile.

"Are they always like that?" Robbie looks at me; his eyes are really big.

"Marquetta says they're just nasty people." I lean forward and peek around the corner. "My dad must be in the kitchen now. He's gonna be busy talking to Mr. Van Horn and waiting on the guests. Marquetta can't leave the kitchen until breakfast is over. So this is perfect. All I gotta do is walk across the lobby, go behind the desk, and grab the key from the third drawer on the right side."

Robbie's jaw drops, and he's staring at me again. "All the rooms have the same key?"

"Doh. No, Robbie, it's a master. Each room has its own key, but the master works on all of them. It's kinda lame. Who still uses real keys in a place like this?"

"Wow." Robbie's eyes are huge now, and he's smiling at me like he's impressed. "You sure know a lot about running a B&B, Alex."

Holy moly, Robbie doesn't give out a lot of compliments. What do I say? I pretend to slug him on the shoulder with my fist. It's like a little tap—I guess it's the kind grownups call a love tap—and change the subject. "When Captain Jack did his big remodel, they didn't have key card locks. Heck, they didn't even have cell phones back in those days. How did they text each other?"

Robbie shakes his head. He doesn't say a word. Typical Robbie. Boys can be so lame.

I take another peek at the dining room. "Piece of cake. I'll go to the front desk."

"Right. What are you waiting for?"

"Morning, Alex."

Holy crap! "Good morning, Miss Kelley." She's right beside me. I smile at her—adorable and innocent—just the way Marquetta does when she's making nice with the guests. "On your way to breakfast?"

"Yes. I'm running late and I'm starved. I can't wait to see what Marquetta has whipped up for us today."

"Awesome." My heart is pounding as she gives us a little wave and goes into the dining room to join the other guests. I mutter, "If she wanted breakfast so bad, why wasn't she on time?"

"Could be she was up to something."

"Let's find out. Lemme get the key."

My heart is racing fast enough to explode as I hurry across the hardwood floors. At the desk, I look around. Nobody.

Check up the stairs. The coast is clear this time. But there are a couple of voices. I can't quite recognize them. And I can barely breathe. Robbie's sitting on the steps giving me a thumbs up. He's got a big smile on his face. How could he not hear those two men?

I can't back out now. I drop down behind the desk and pull open the drawer. There's the key. I grab it, check the lobby one more time, and run back to where Robbie's sitting. I can't let him see how scared I am, so I ignore the voices upstairs and give him another slug on the shoulder. "That was a total rush."

"Awesome."

Robbie's voice is really shaky. He looks like he's gonna puke. Heck, that's the way I feel. What's he all worried about? I'm the one who stole the key. Maybe he's thinking about the men upstairs. He might be pretending not to hear them. I reach out and tug on his hand. He gets up and stands next to me.

My breath catches and now I'm totally gonna throw up. "Come on."

"You are so cool, Alex."

And now my face feels like it's on fire. Holy moly. My stomach's doing flip-flops and...and..

"What's that?" Robbie asks.

"Oh, crap. Breakfast. They're breaking up."

19

RICK

The low din of arguing guests emanating from the dining room grew in intensity. To Rick, it almost sounded like they were getting ready for a full-blown fistfight. Great. That's all they needed, more mayhem.

Ignoring the noise, Marquetta went to the coffeemaker, poured a mug, and handed it to Devon. "And here I thought you stopped by for a shot of this."

"Well, that was kind of on my mind." The big man glanced at the butler's door and winced. He raised his mug to toast, but his gaze returned to the sounds of the argument. "Here's to the best coffee in Seaside Cove."

"I need to squelch this," Rick said.

"I've got it." Marquetta picked up a tray on which there were two carafes, a water pitcher, and a small supply of sugar and creamer. "You two should talk." She backed out the butler door and winked at them. With the door open, it sounded like a wall of sound blasted into the kitchen.

"Thanks," Rick mumbled. He was in no shape to deal with cranky guests, but was it any better to be forced into fending off Devon's gossip-seeking urges? That wasn't exactly easy either.

Still, Marquetta was already gone and Devon was all his. Or was it the other way around?

The sound of Marquetta clearing her throat in the other room carried easily through the door. It reminded Rick of a kindergarten teacher bringing order to her class. The guests quieted, and Rick was mystified by how she'd pulled that off. He leaned sideways against the kitchen island and gazed at Devon.

"What's the damage?"

"Nobody messes with Marquetta," Devon shook his head, sipped from his mug, and smacked his lips. "Sweet as pie and tough as a marine drill sergeant. Yessir, I don't want to cross her."

"Me either," Rick said.

"And she makes the best coffee. What's her secret ingredient?"

Not again. More drivel? "Really, Devon? I had a late night and an early morning."

"I guess she won't tell you, huh?"

Oh, good God. "Yes, everyone loves Marquetta's coffee. No, I don't know what her secret ingredient is because...because it's a secret."

Devon's smile drooped, and he shrugged. "Can't blame a guy for trying." A moment later, his cheerful attitude was back. "So, late night? What happened?"

Just what he suspected. Devon's visit did have something to do with the midnight callout to Deputy Cunningham. Without a doubt, Devon had discovered what happened and was fishing for juicy news. "I've been trying to get that estimate for a week. I'd rather stay focused on the B&B. My head is killing me."

"Oh." Devon glanced away for a moment and grimaced. "I'm sorry if I seemed pushy."

Now he'd offended his handyman. This was not starting off to be a good day. Rick shook his head and lowered his voice, determined to repair any damage he might have done. "As much as I'd like to, I can't really discuss last night. You know how it is, ongoing investigation. That sort of thing."

It took a few seconds, but Devon's eyes soon lit up. "Oh, you're working with the law. That's different. Well, let's stick to business in that case. The estimate is somewhere between five hundred and twenty-five hundred." He shrugged and continued. "Sorry I can't be more specific. The reason for such a wide range is this is either a really straightforward job or a very tricky one. And we won't know until I get into it. Here, look at this."

Rick set down his coffee and did his best to focus as Devon held out his phone and scrolled through a few photos.

"This is the pulley system." Devon flicked his index finger to the left. "This is the elevator shaft. See that construction? It's antiquated. Captain Jack ignored it. I can't count the number of times I told him it needed maintenance, but he would never put out the money. It looks like you're the guy who's stuck with the repairs."

"Wait. We were talking about the back stairs. How does the dumbwaiter fit into this?"

"That's what I was showing you." Devon scrolled back one photo. "The stairs are on the other side of this wall. The minute I cut into it, this cross member could be compromised. The bottom line is, doing anything on those stairs will mean we could be messing with the shaft and its supports. It's all original materials, so the wood is dry and brittle."

Rick sighed as the weight of the morning crushed his spirit. "This is that touch one thing and something else breaks problem, isn't it?"

"It's hundred-year-old construction. You're lucky this place isn't on the historic register. It would cost ten times as much to change a lightbulb. Don't be surprised if we surface a host of other problems. There's no telling what will happen when I open everything up."

Just like Gordon's murder. One thing led to another. Rick stared at the screen on Devon's phone, unable to avert his eyes from the sight of the ancient equipment. Could he ever catch a break? Would Captain Jack's "grand remodel" ever stop haunting him?

"This is plain ugly, Devon."

"That's nothing. There's the kids to consider."

"Kids? What—oh, God no. Don't tell me there was an accident."

"Nope." Devon grinned from ear-to-ear, then averted his gaze. When he looked back at Rick, he sighed and continued. "First off, nobody ever got trapped, but me and every kid who was raised in Seaside Cove took at least one ride in it."

"Why would anybody in their right mind want to..." His voice trailed off as an image of Alex and Robbie popped into his head. Oh, no, they were alone. "My daughter and a friend are upstairs. I should check on them."

"You might be better off keeping this quiet for now."

"Is it really that much of a thrill ride?"

Devon snickered. "There aren't a lot of exciting things to do in Seaside Cove."

"I can't believe this."

No, he could. His daughter was fearless. And Robbie would do anything she asked him to. She loved climbing the old oak in the side yard. And if she learned about this—who's to say she hadn't— she'd be first in line for a ride.

"Okay, it's a safety hazard," he said. "We need to do something to seal it up."

Devon cleared his throat. "Right. It's not safe at all these days. I remember Captain Jack chewing my rear end on a bunch of—uh, when I took my ride."

"I think you left off the plural."

"Right. Rides. He was pretty doggone upset at the time. The shaft and equipment were safe in those days. Back then the place was in tiptop condition." Devon winked. "I always thought Captain Jack just liked being ornery."

Didn't that sound exactly like Captain Jack? "Let's keep this on the QT. Okay?"

"No worries, Rick. She's not going to hear about it from me."

The butler door swung open and Marquetta burst in carrying a tray with the empty water pitcher and a few dirty glasses. She asked, "Hear about what?"

"The dumbwaiter," Devon said.

"Oh my God," Marquetta laughed. "That was the most fun I've ever had in my life! I can't count how many times Captain Jack let me ride that when I was little."

Rick stared at her. So did Devon.

"What?" Marquetta shrugged, then walked across the room to the sink. She set down the tray, turned to face the two men and said, "What a couple of old grumps."

20

ALEX

"I thought we were gonna get busted, but Marquetta's got everything under control. Let's go." I wave for Robbie to follow me.

"Awesome!" We fist bump as we climb the stairs, then he whispers to me. "I never spied before."

Me neither. We pass a couple more guests on the way up. It's the two men we heard when we were downstairs. "Good morning, Mr. Luhan. Good morning, Mr. Joshua."

They both kinda grunt and ignore us.

At the top landing, Robbie tugs on my T-shirt sleeve. "They're really nasty, aren't they?"

"Awful." One last peek down the stairs. It's quiet. And Marquetta's keeping the guests under control. She's so strong. It makes me sad cause I'm doing something she won't like. But I gotta do this to help Daddy.

Now, Robbie's looking kinda queasy, too. Like he's chickening out. I grab his hand again. "Come on. I wanna check out Miss Kelley's room first."

"Wait. Are you sure about this, Alex? Isn't it against the law to go busting into people's rooms? Could we go to jail if we get caught?"

His blue eyes make me go all mushy inside. I haven't told Robbie yet, but we're gonna get married when we grow up.

"Nah, my dad owns the B&B." I totally stretch the truth to calm Robbie down. "We can go into anybody's room whenever we want. We just gotta tell them we're coming in. That's why we keep the master key downstairs. In case we need it. The key gives us permission to go into any room."

"Whoa...any of them?"

"Well, not my dad's office cause he's got a special key. But any of the guest rooms are cool. C'mon, let's get into Miss Kelley's. Maybe we can prove who killed Mr. Gordon."

I stuff the key into my jeans and grab Robbie's hand. He tags along behind me. When we get to the Quarter Deck room, Robbie steps forward.

"Lemme do it." He holds his hand out.

"We gotta knock first."

He glances at where we were a minute ago. "Isn't she the lady who passed us on her way downstairs?"

"It's the rule, Robbie."

He scrunches up his face and shrugs. "Okay." Then, he knocks.

Miss Kelley doesn't answer.

Robbie stares at me. "Now what?"

I hold out the key for him to take, but I'm the one who stole it, and I don't want him getting blamed for this. All of a sudden, I think I might chicken out. My stomach's queasy. If we don't do something fast, we're gonna get caught cause Daddy and Marquetta are coming. I can hear them talking. They must be near the top of the stairs and just around the corner. If they see us—I shove the key in the lock and twist.

Holy cow. It worked.

"Alex," Robbie hisses. "Your dad's coming."

I know. I know! My heart is racing. We're gonna be in so much trouble for this. But I gotta help Daddy. The voices are almost at the corner.

I shove the door open. Pull Robbie in. Shut the door.

We stand there, staring at each other. Is Robbie's heart racing like mine? His face is all splotchy.

"That was awesome," he whispers.

He's breathless. Me, too. I can barely speak. "We made it."

"That was close." Robbie's mouth is hanging open. Then he starts to smile. "We totally did it." He looks around the room and his jaw drops again. "Alex, she's, like, a total neat freak. How are we gonna find anything in here?"

"She must be hiding it."

"What?"

He's right. I got no idea what we're looking for, and she put all her stuff away. None of the stuff I expected. "This sucks." The only thing I see is an envelope on the nightstand. It's not sealed. My heart is pounding a million miles a minute. This is a major rush.

"Should we read it?" Robbie asks.

"Yeah, we should read it."

"Yeah." Robbie doesn't sound too sure either.

My fingers are shaking so bad when I pick up the envelope that I almost drop it. "It smells like a lady's perfume."

Robbie sniffs and wrinkles his nose. "It stinks."

"It's perfume, Robbie." Boys. "Holy cow, it's a love letter."

My darling,

I am so sorry for the way I've been acting. I was jealous of your relationship with Reese and how close you two have become. My trust in you is unequivocal.

Yours always,

Monica

"What's that mean, Alex?"

"Un-equiv...I don't know."

"It's just mushy stuff. Let's go."

I get the note in the envelope and put it back where we found it. Robbie's already at the door. He looks scared.

"What if there's somebody in the hall?"

Oh, man, I never thought about the getaway. "We'll have to go for it."

I open the door real slow and Robbie sticks his head out. When he turns around, he says, "We're in the clear."

"Awesome. We got time for one more."

Robbie's eyes are so big they might pop out of his head. "I dunno, Alex. I'm kinda worried."

"We can't chicken out now, Robbie. We gotta help my dad. Let's check Mr. Santiago's room. He's not very nice, either."

Entering the room is easier this time and when we're in we go straight to the desk on the far wall. "Score!" We do another high five.

Mr. Santiago's not a neat person at all. He leaves his stuff laying around. "Look at that, Robbie! It's a notebook."

"Whoa...awesome. What do you think it's for?"

"It's probably his journal. Marquetta says journals are for your innermost thoughts."

"Inner what? You mean he might confess in here?"

I didn't think of that. Me and Robbie start looking through the pages. "This is weird. It's not like mi—a regular journal." Robbie doesn't know I keep one. I'm not sure I want to tell him. "He doesn't write in here. These are just news clippings and pictures."

"Totally weird," Robbie says. "It's kinda like the album my mom used to keep."

He sounds really sad when he says that. So sad I'm not sure if I can ask what he means. Instead, I finger the journal. "Let's see how far back it goes."

We start flipping pages and it doesn't take long to get to the beginning. "Look, it's a news story and a photo. This is from, like, three years ago." I point at the men in the picture. "That's Mr. Santiago. And he's with Mr. Gordon."

"The dead guy? Alex, why's the dead guy got an X through his face?"

"I dunno. This says Mr. Gordon found some treasure with Mr. Santiago's help." A couple more pages and we see another one. "He really had a thing about Mr. Gordon."

"There's one more."

"Wow. He must have, like, at least ten of these. We could..." I stop talking and grip Robbie's arm.

The muffled voice outside calls me again. "Alex? Where are you?"

Robbie starts to answer, but I cover his mouth with my hand. "Shhh."

"It's Marquetta!" I whisper. "She's looking for us." Oh, man, this is so not good.

Her voice gets louder. "Alex? Robbie? Are you up here?"

Poor Robbie looks like he's gonna pee his pants. Me, too. I'm gonna be grounded for life if Marquetta finds out what we're up to.

"She'll go downstairs if we don't answer. We'll meet her in the lobby. It's cool."

A few seconds later, Marquetta's gone and I can't hear any sounds in the hallway. Robbie checks. The hallway's empty. We get the door closed and run to the stairs. Marquetta's at the bottom. She must hear us cause she turns around.

"Alex?" She gets that scrunchy look on her face. "Where have you been? I've been looking all over for you."

"We were playing hide-and-seek." I feel awful lying to her, but she'll be super mad if she finds out what we did.

She's looking at me like she doesn't believe me. Her eyes dart over at Robbie, then back to me. It's like she can see right through me. I'm totally gonna lose it if she keeps staring at me.

"Well, it's time for breakfast and a little baking. In the kitchen, you two."

Me and Robbie glance at each other. We do a quick high five behind Marquetta's back. She stops, turns, and looks at us again. Then, she turns away and pushes through the butler door.

Holy cow. That was close.

21

RICK

Marquetta sliced a loaf of zucchini bread onto a serving platter, then pulled a pitcher of orange juice from the refrigerator. She placed both on a tray and headed for the butler door. She backed through the door with the tray balanced in her hands. "This won't take long."

"I can't believe Captain Jack let her ride the dumbwaiter," Devon grumbled.

"There was a very unusual relationship between her and my grandfather."

Devon gazed off to one side for a few moments. How was this even possible? His handyman had nothing to say? He always had something. "Come on, you know you want to tell me."

There was a heavy sigh, and Devon's normally cheery smile dissolved. He said, "There's a story there, but it's not mine to tell. Let's talk about your repairs."

"They come at a really bad time."

"I know." The handyman nodded and gazed around the room. "Captain Jack's big remodel was mostly cosmetic. He ignored the bones. It's been many a year since the B&B was in tip-top condition. The bottom line is he let the infrastructure maintenance slide to help finance the facelift. The old girl needs some TLC."

"Can we secure the dumbwaiter for now? Maybe seal it off? What would that cost?"

"Depends on how bad you want the walls to look. If we start talking about finish work, you might as well put the money into repairs."

Raucous laughter came from the dining room, bringing with it a sense of insecurity. What if someone burst in? Rick didn't want any interruptions. He glanced at Devon. "For once, they're not fighting. Let's step outside."

"Great idea."

Devon grinned at Rick like a little boy caught with his hand in a cookie jar as he refilled his mug. They went out to the patio and Devon headed straight for one of the Adirondack chairs. Rick had no intention of spending the morning sitting around exchanging idle gossip, but something Devon said had him intrigued. He considered how to proceed.

"Before you get too comfortable, I only have a few minutes. This is our busiest time of the day and I can't put all the work on Marquetta. And something tells me you didn't come here just to deliver the quote. I can't really talk much, so..."

Devon raised a bear-paw like hand. "You're right on all counts, but this is something you need to know. Rumor has it Marquetta's leaving."

"What?" Rick's jaw dropped. "Where did that come from? When?"

"So it's not true?"

Rick's heart pounded. Was that why she'd been so upset this morning? Should he ask her? What if it was just another rumor? "Tell me where you heard that. It's not true. Not at all."

"Okay, sounds like the rumor mill got the old wires crossed. Glad to know." He grinned and made a clicking sound. "I like to clear these kinds of things up to quell the fires. You understand, right?"

What he understood was Devon mainlined gossip. In fact, it appeared Seaside Cove was loaded with juicy-news junkies. The bigger problem was how would he ever find a handyman who wasn't a gossip? Firing Devon and bringing in someone from San Ladron, which was a much larger city and nearly an hour's drive, would be tantamount to cutting himself off from the local business community. Nope. Not even a remote option. "No worries, Devon," Rick lied. "I get it."

"Can I ask you one more question?"

Why not? Rick still had some of his own. Especially now that he'd found out the rumor about Marquetta leaving. "Sure."

"I understand you called Adam out in the middle of the night to arrest Mr. Richardson."

"That just happened a few hours ago." Rick narrowed his eyes and stared at Devon until he looked away. He suppressed the desire to express his suspicions about the real reason for this visit, but stopped himself. Instead, he feigned surprise. "It's hard to believe you heard about it already."

Devon laughed nervously. "We have an efficient system here in Seaside Cove." He glanced up with a sheepish smile. "So what really happened?"

Now Rick really was trapped. Not telling the whole story would only make things worse. The gossip junkies would start passing around the news and he would become part of the problem. If he refused to answer altogether, Devon might stonewall him when it was time for Rick to ask his own questions.

"I'm really limited by what I can discuss. I'm sure you understand. But, there was no arrest. There was never any intention of having him arrested. Mr. Richardson told us he was retrieving his monopod after he took some sunset photos. Because it was near the spot where Mr. Gordon died, I thought it best if Adam took it in as evidence."

Devon grimaced. "These so-called treasure seekers." He sighed and laid a hand on Rick's shoulder. "Look, I really do have a reason for asking about this."

"And that is?"

"Do you have any idea what these guests of yours do?" Devon peered at Rick. "I mean, it takes a lot of expertise to track down a prize like a sunken Spanish galleon. What do they bring to the table? There are an awful lot of wannabes who show up in this town looking for a big score."

That assumed the treasure was even real. After his conversation with Reese, Rick wasn't sure about that, either. "I have no idea what background they have. They're registered guests. I saw one of the invitations. It looked legitimate. But I have no interest in checking them out. It's not my place to evaluate why people stay with us."

"I understand, but you should go talk to Lungs. He knows all this stuff."

Rick shrugged and leaned back a little as he focused on Devon. "Lungs? What are you talking about?"

"Not what, who. I guess nobody's told you about Joe Gray. He runs Gray's Sailing Charters. We been calling him Lungs since grade school. He learned to free dive almost before he could walk. He stayed down once for fifteen minutes."

"That's impossible," Rick snorted.

"Nope." Devon winked at him. "World record is more than twenty. Anyway, go talk to Lungs. He's done a bunch of dives for treasure himself. Guy's an expert. If anybody around here can give you some background, it'll be him."

What Rick hated to admit out loud was that he was curious about the *San Manuel*—and he did want to confirm Reese's story. "So Joe is the expert on treasure? How long has he been doing this?"

"Long time. He used to dive for Neal Weiss."

"Who's he?"

"Oh, you don't know. Marquetta's father."

Rick's breath caught in his throat. It was almost as though Devon had read his thoughts. Rick couldn't believe his luck. "How long ago was this?"

"They were pretty tight until the day Neal died. I see where you're going. You don't want to do this. Do not ask him about Marquetta." Devon shook his head. "That's not why I recommended him."

Really? If there was some big secret surrounding Marquetta, why had Devon mentioned Joe Gray at all? Besides, Rick had so many questions. About the treasure hunters, sure. But what if he could help Marquetta move beyond the emotional hump she seemed to be stuck on? Even though the possibility might be slim, he had to try.

Rick licked his lips and looked at Devon. "She's always said her life is not a subject for debate or discussion."

"It's not. She's very particular about that."

"Why?"

"I told you. It's not my story to tell."

Rick's throat felt dry as he thought about the warning. But, more than anything, he wanted to learn what dark secret prevented Marquetta from talking about her past. If Joe Gray helped him understand, he might be able to help her get past whatever obstacles she faced.

For the first time this morning, it seemed as though a weight had been lifted from Rick's shoulders. He smiled at the big man. "Thank you, Devon. I mean that. I'll talk to him later."

Devon's shoulders slumped as he stood. "I have to go." He walked away before Rick could respond.

22

RICK

Rick walked left on Front Street, then turned onto Ferry Dock Road. The Seaside Cove Harbor was at the end of the road. Gray's Sailing Charters was in a double-decker houseboat. It had teak paneling with teal-painted accents and white trim. A bank of large windows lined the second deck.

The front door, a decorative wood with an etched-glass window set in, stood open. Rick entered and the man behind the counter glanced up. His blue eyes sparkled with youthful exuberance. In contrast, his face bore lines from years of exposure to the elements and his once-sandy hair had silvered, probably many years before.

Rick waved and extended his hand as he approached. "You must be Joe Gray."

"Yessir. And you're Rick Atwood. My wife talks about you all the time." The man placed a gold coin and white cloth on the countertop and pulled off the cotton glove covering his right hand.

The first thought that popped into Rick's head was his discussion with Marquetta about the twenty-two mothers who wanted him as a son-in-law. "She does?" He couldn't help but wonder where Joe's wife fell in that grouping. Probably Doers. He forced a nervous laugh as they shook hands. "Do I want to know what she's saying?"

"No worries, Rick. I saw that look of panic. Yes, I do have a daughter, but she's got a good career as a medical technician in San Francisco."

"So she doesn't live here? Oh, sorry. That didn't come out the way I meant."

Joe laughed. "It's okay. If I were in your shoes, I'd be gun-shy, too. Obviously, you're familiar with the town marriage competition. My wife doesn't like to accept it, but Sally's perfectly happy being single and working. I'd love to be a grandpa someday soon, but kids have to do things in their own time."

At last. A voice of reason from a parent in Seaside Cove. What a relief. "I hope you get your wish," Rick said.

"Me, too. It would take away the tension when Sally visits. Unfortunately, you're probably not here to discuss a marriage proposal. My best guess is one of your guests needs a charter, but I thought Adam put them all under house arrest."

Joe might be a voice of reason, but he obviously had his hooks in the rumor mill, too. "That's not really true. They're free to come and go as they please. Adam did ask them to not leave town though."

"Oh?" The blue eyes flashed with interest.

"It's standard procedure in a murder." Rick flipped one hand nonchalantly. "It's a precaution in case further questioning is needed."

"And Adam didn't take one of them in?"

"That was Mr. Richardson. And he did ask him to update his statement."

"Well...interesting. Thanks for the clarification."

"No problem."

"You must want a boat, then," Joe said.

"The guests are looking for a sunken Spanish galleon."

"Aren't they all?"

Rick shook his head and stared at Joe. "I don't understand."

"Half my business comes from treasure hunters." Joe's blue eyes flicked over to a picture on the wall. A young woman in a black cap and gown smiled at the camera. "Gotta love 'em. They put Sally through college." He turned back to Rick. "Which one are they looking for this time?"

"The *San Manuel.*"

Joe harrumphed as he pulled on the white glove and picked up the coin he'd placed on the counter earlier.

"Those look pretty old," Rick said.

"They are." Joe examined the coin and set it inside the glass display case next to four others. They were all lined up in a neat row. "From my younger days."

"Nice. That one looks familiar."

Joe rested his finger about an inch above the coin Rick had indicated. "It's a twenty-dollar Liberty gold piece. It was quite a find." He closed the back of the case and pulled off the glove. "But, you're not here to admire my little coin collection. The *San Manuel*—that's the sunken ship Francine was talking about. Never heard of it before. Based on the story she rattled off, it sounds pretty implausible."

"How do you know?"

"I'm somewhat of a history buff—especially the nautical variety. Too many of the facts in Francine's little tale don't mesh with historical fact. Of course, knowing Francine, she might have embellished the details in her version."

Rick chuckled. "Point taken." The Mayor was, if nothing else, confident in her interpretation of the world. He rested one elbow on the case. "What did she say?"

"Something about a Dutch navigator working with a Spanish captain—the thing is, the Dutch were busy with a revolt around that time. Same old thing. In those days, it was the Protestants not being happy with the Catholic crown."

"Some things never change," Rick said.

"Only the names." Joe paused and leaned forward on both elbows. "The route for the Incan gold would have taken them south, not north. Even the most inexperienced captain would have turned around long before they got to California. No. I just can't buy it."

"I've got eight guests—make that seven—who are convinced this thing is real. Could there be something they know—maybe some previously undiscovered detail—that you don't?"

"Sure. There are all sorts of possibilities. I'm not saying it couldn't happen. To me though, the whole thing is simply not believable. The fact is, it's easy to get eight people to believe in something no matter how bogus it is."

With that, Rick had to agree, but just because the experts defined a set of "facts" didn't make them correct, either. It wasn't a point Rick wanted to argue. "Tell me something, Joe. You're the second person today who's quizzed me about the murder. It must be all over the local grapevine. What are they saying?"

"Murder's a big deal here. It just doesn't happen. Oddly enough, there's surprisingly little on it. Devon seems to have the most."

"I'll tell you the same thing I told him, which is I can't talk about an ongoing investigation."

"No worries." Joe winked and gave Rick a sly smile. "I see Devon at Bayside Coffee most mornings. You should stop in sometime. It's quite the little hotspot."

Rick flinched at the memory of his conversation with Devon. He'd let slip the story about the monopod and why he'd called out Adam. Even rationalized that he was helping to quell rumors, not spread them. But he hadn't counted on people warping the facts and now that information was working its way through the town.

"It sounds like the news is moving faster than the truth," Rick said.

"You want me to tell you what I heard?"

"If you wouldn't mind."

Joe's smile broadened as he leaned forward. When he was done, a sense of relief came over Rick. The rumor had the facts mostly correct.

"There's only one thing wrong," Rick said, "Mr. Richardson wasn't arrested. He was merely questioned."

"Got it," Joe said. "I'll be sure to pass it along."

Rick suppressed a snicker. He was confident Joe would be on the phone at the first available moment. He also resolved to ask Marquetta who the big town gossips were. He already knew about Francine, Devon, and Joe Gray. How many more were out there lurking? His pulse quickened. Could he get away with a white lie about his real reason for being here? Perhaps. What did he have to lose?

23

RICK

Rick considered his options one last time. If he launched into questions about Marquetta's father, Joe might not answer, and Marquetta would probably find out what he'd done. No, he had to continue the ruse.

"We kind of got off track. With your background, it sounds like yours is the best place to find my guests a boat for their little excursion."

"Happy to help. I've seen a bunch of these treasure hunters come and go. Right now the weather is good—no storms in sight. My schedule's clear if they want to go out in the next day or two. In another couple of weeks I'll be swamped, so this works out well."

Amazing, Joe showed no signs of having heard from Devon. It appeared the handyman was, for now, keeping their discussion private. Which meant Rick could finish this ruse and get to his real purpose in coming here.

"I'll be sure to let them know. Have you had much success—finding treasure, that is?"

Joe shrugged and his upper lip curled. "Most of the people coming here fail. They're amateurs who rely more on luck and prayers than solid information. There have been a few successes, but even for the ones who show up prepared, they still need luck and good fortune."

Rick burst out laughing. "That's what I've been doing wrong. I always thought those two were the same. I need some of both right now."

"It would be good fortune to have a reliable map. They'll still need some luck to actually find a sunken ship."

"That whole thing is strange. They each have one part of— well, it looks like a nautical chart or something." Rick proceeded to described how each guest had received an invitation along with their individual map section.

"Somebody cut it up?" Joe blinked and his jaw dropped. "You can't be serious. How old is it?"

"I'm not sure. The paper's yellowed and looks brittle. I'm no expert, but it sure appears to be an antique. If you buy what they're saying, it's from the sixteenth century."

Joe's thin eyebrows narrowed. "Strangest thing I've ever heard." He stared down at the coins in his display case. "Why would anybody in their right mind deface a valuable artifact like that? It's either a fake or these people don't have a lick of sense."

"I kind of hoped you'd enlighten me about it. Or maybe the legend."

"No can do." Joe raised his palms and shook his head. "Even if you had one of those map sections, I'm not the guy to talk to. You want Howie Dockham. He owns Howie's Collectibles. Worked for some big east coast museum as a curator before he retired here. Howie's a good guy. Loves this kind of stuff. He uses the shop to keep himself occupied during the day."

"I've seen it, but I'm not sure we've ever met."

"You can't miss the guy. He has the motorized wheelchair with the big flag. His big thrill is racing the tourists at the intersections."

"Oh, him. We have met." Rick crossed his arms over his chest. "He almost ran me down. I wasn't too happy with him at the time."

"That's Howie. For a stamp collector who can't walk, you might say he's pretty adventurous." Joe chuckled and gave a firm nod of his head. "Check with him. He knows his stuff."

As the conversation wound down, Rick's anxiety grew. He still had the big question he wanted to ask. He'd passed on a couple of opportunities to weave it in and now he'd run out of questions. Out of time. Misgivings or not, he had to ask what this man knew or give up. "You said you worked with different treasure hunters over the years."

"Some very good ones." Joe let out a wistful sigh.

"Was one of those Neal Weiss?"

"Good man. Shame, the way he died." Joe turned to study a picture on the wall of two men. Grief crept into Joe's eyes. He ran a hand through his silvered hair. "I'm surprised Marky told you about him."

One of the men in the photo was obviously a younger version of the man before him; Rick supposed the other might be Neal Weiss. They stood on the docks in front of a boat that reminded Rick of a fishing trawler. He bit his tongue. Did he tell another lie? Confess his reason for this visit? Instead, he waited.

"You need to give Marky a little space right now." Joe cleared his throat. "We're coming up on the anniversary of her father's death."

An uncomfortable heat rushed into Rick's cheeks. Why hadn't he ever asked her about this? Yes, he thought—her, not others. But, like a moth drawn to a flame, he couldn't stop himself. "Is that why she's been on edge lately?"

"Might not have been so bad, but this group you've got here—it must be bringing back a lot of memories. Neal was a top-notch seaman. He had a fifty-foot boat and a seasoned crew. He made a small fortune taking treasure hunters out on all sorts of expeditions. It's just like your guests, they get word about these legends or find some doodling on a napkin and the next thing you know they're gambling away their life savings hoping fate will smile on them."

Rick shot another glance at the picture of the men in front of the boat—which didn't look like a fishing trawler at all. There were no nets. No poles or lines. It had to be for excursions. "Marquetta said he was chasing treasure all the time."

"Neal had the fever, all right. He developed quite a name for himself. On his last expedition, he had two divers, a maritime archaeologist, and a boatload of state-of-the-art equipment. There was a ton of money being thrown at him."

"Sounds like he was a lot more professional than this group."

"He was one of the best, but he's the reason I say even the good ones need a healthy dose of luck. The thing about luck is that it's fickle. And toward the end, Lady Luck was not smiling on Neal Weiss. Call it what you want, things were starting to go wrong. It got so bad his backers threatened to pull out."

Was this Marquetta's secret? Something so simple as her father failing? "What happened?"

"They gave him a fool's errand—find the treasure or lose your reputation." Joe closed his eyes and sighed. "He started taking chances, but still came home empty. The backers gave him one final ultimatum, so he went out despite heavy seas. He knew better. So did his crew. But they believed in him—and he believed in himself."

With his heart in his throat, Rick waited and watched as Joe stared at the photo. The older man blanched as though memories were flooding his thoughts. Rick knew the feeling well.

After a long breath, Joe wiped his cheek and sniffled. "It was a bitter day. Windy. Cold. Rain coming and going. Despite that, half the town turned out. I'll never forget Marquetta out there at the very edge of the docks. Heartbreaking. I can see her now— this little girl standing next to her mother waving goodbye to her daddy. A man she'd never see again."

Joe sniffled and swiped at his cheek. "God himself couldn't have conducted a safe dive in weather like that, but Neal and his crew were determined. They were the best, and they felt they were invincible. But by the end of that day, every member of that crew was bone tired, and they still had nothing. The seas were treacherous. Neal had one diver left in the water when he pulled the plug on the operation. He was helping his diver climb on board when a wave caught them sideways. Neal was washed overboard."

Rick stared at Joe. Cold gripped his heart. There was no way to stop it. All he could think of was poor Marquetta. And what he couldn't say to her the next time he saw her.

24

RICK

A lone seagull's haunting caw drifted through the open window, breaking the silence inside the cabin of Joe Gray's houseboat. Tiny wavelets slapping against the sides shushed the air and Rick sensed the boat swaying ever-so-slightly. Treasure—Neal Weiss had died chasing it. Suddenly, Rick understood so much more.

"How old was Marquetta when this happened?"

"Ten."

Rick's stomach clenched, unable to shake the vision. He could see her. A little girl. She stood alone. Tears streamed down her cheeks while she watched the sea for a man who would never return. Maybe Devon was right. Why wouldn't Marquetta leave with that memory haunting her? Seaside Cove held too much pain. "It's no wonder she's such a cynic about these treasure hunts."

Joe nodded first, but shook his head as he spoke. "She's never really gotten over the loss." He cleared his throat. "Every now and again, I still see her down here. Though it's been a lot less lately. Anyway, treasure is how we all make money in Seaside Cove. And Marky's a tough girl. She'll push through this, eventually."

Eventually. Big word, thought Rick. And it had been fifteen years since her father died. Like the moth, Rick had gotten too close to the flame. Of that, he was sure.

He let out a slow breath and glanced at the clock on the wall. Lots of brass. Roman numerals for the hours. Very nautical, like everything else here. It was nine-thirty. Time to make his exit. "That's a nice clock. And it reminds me I need to be getting back to work."

"No worries." Joe reached across the case to shake Rick's hand. "Hope I've helped."

"Thank you. I've learned a lot."

He waved goodbye and left, but on the walk home, the image of that little girl waiting for her father kept intruding into his thoughts. When he made the turn onto Front Street, he saw Mayor Carter standing on the front porch of the B&B. She would probably tell him she wasn't happy about Adam's callout last night. Or chew him out for getting the body moved. There were more possibilities than he could count.

Francine waved when she spotted him and hurried down the stairs. She was still a good ten feet away when she started in. "Rick, there are a number of people in this town who care a great deal about you and your daughter."

Oh, great, this was going to be a doozy. Francine was in politician mode—start sweet, drive the knife in deep, leave with a compliment. He resisted the urge to call the mayor on her standard device. Instead, he said, "That's nice to know."

"I should be mad at you," she continued. "However, I fully understand why you went above my head. In fact, I respect you for it."

The mayor? Respected him? What kind of trick was this? Francine never liked being left out of the loop. "We needed to secure the body."

"No. Enough said. What's done is done. Last night you did what you thought was right, and that's what's important. After all, what life lesson would you be teaching your daughter if she saw you not standing up for yourself?"

"Well, Madame Mayor, thank you, but I'm sure you didn't walk all the way over here just to tell me that."

"On this visit, I'm merely Francine Carter, humble proprietor of Scoops & Scones. This morning while opening up, I discovered this lying on the sidewalk in front of my store. Why none of my customers from yesterday mentioned it, I have no idea. Quite likely, it sat out all night long on the sidewalk. However, it belongs to Mr. Richardson. I'm surprised he hasn't missed it."

Rick glanced down at a brown leather wallet Francine held out. "Mr. Richardson has been somewhat preoccupied. He's quite forgetful. If you'd like, I'll return it to him."

"Marvelous." Francine handed the wallet to Rick and chirped, "My customers await!" She left, waving goodbye over her head as she bustled along Front Street.

"What a surprise," he whispered to himself. The mayor had actually complimented him for doing something right. He looked briefly at the open front door before turning back to the street. Francine might be gone, but her comment about what his actions taught Alex still hung in the air. What would his visit to Joe Gray teach her? It's okay to go behind someone's back? It was not a lesson he wanted to teach his daughter.

If Marquetta didn't want him to learn about her past, he wouldn't pry again. He vowed to tread lightly around her and not say another word until she broached the subject. On his way into the house, Rick met Hayden. They exchanged greetings, comments about the lovely day, and then Hayden asked if Rick knew when they'd be free to leave.

"I don't. That's up to Deputy Cunningham. But, while I think of it, I do have one question about something Monica said."

"In that case, why don't you ask her?"

"Because it concerns you."

"Oh. What do you want to know?"

"You gave Mr. Gordon CPR when you found the body. Is that correct?"

"I did. Wasn't easy to do on those rocks, either."

"Exactly. I've been wondering how you accomplished that."

Hayden fidgeted with the collar of his leather jacket. "I don't want to make a big deal of it."

"Then there's the position of the body."

Giving a quick shake of his head, Hayden raised both eyebrows and stared at Rick. "Huh?"

"When I got there, the body was face down. But, for you to give CPR it had to be face up."

Hayden looked stunned.

"Well?" Rick peered at him. "How did you give CPR when the body was in a position that would have made it impossible? Please, Mr. Kalstone, I'd love to hear how you pulled it off."

There was a long pause during which Hayden closed his eyes and hung his head. "Okay, okay. Monica was mistaken. I wasn't giving Jim CPR."

"How did she get the idea you were?"

"I might have...told her that's what I was doing."

"And you did that because..."

"I, um, can't really say."

"You perpetuated the lie with Deputy Cunningham. Why did you lead him to believe the same thing?"

"Monica told him what I did first. Besides, it's not like I committed perjury or anything."

"Actually, you did."

Hayden groaned, crossed his arms over his chest, and mumbled something to himself.

"What was that, Mr. Kalstone?"

He sighed. "I don't even know how you do CPR."

25

RICK

Rick dialed Deputy Cunningham's cell. He watched Hayden's face as the phone rang. "We'll need to get the deputy out here so you can give him a new statement. And this time you'll tell the full truth. Right?"

"Sure thing." Hayden grimaced. "I'll correct it with him."

Rick told the deputy what had happened, then escorted Hayden inside and locked Cadman's wallet in the house safe. He instructed Hayden to wait in the lobby while he went to see if Marquetta needed help. The aroma of baking cookie dough hung in the air. Was that chocolate he smelled also? He hoped she was making his favorite, chocolate chip cookies.

In the kitchen, Alex stood in front of the oven, her eyes glued to the timer. Robbie was next to Marquetta at the sink. She handed Robbie a wooden spoon to dry. The boy wore a flour-dusted apron smeared with several dark splotches and chocolate smudges around his mouth. Obviously, Robbie wasn't the neatest little baker, but he appeared to be doing an acceptable job of helping with the cleanup.

"Three minutes," Alex said as she peeked into the oven.

"And counting," Marquetta shot back. "Robbie, let's put you over here." She guided the boy to one of the barstools and patted the one next to it. "Sweetie, you don't need to watch those every second. Come sit here with Robbie."

Alex's shoulders slumped, and she glanced at Rick. "Hi, Daddy." She left her post and positioned herself between the barstool and Marquetta. "I'm your official cookie tester, right?"

"I don't think so, it's too close to lunch." Marquetta put her hands on Alex's waist and gave her a boost up. She helped straighten the girl's shorts and pink tank top. "You're getting way too heavy for me."

"Please? Just one?"

Robbie raised one finger and grinned from ear-to-ear, too.

Despite Alex's huge smile, Marquetta resisted with a mild frown. Alex countered with an exaggerated pout. She had her hair pulled back in a ponytail, much like Marquetta's, and Rick was sure of what would come next. He snickered as Marquetta winced and leaned forward. She kissed Alex on the forehead and glanced at him.

"You'll have to ask your dad."

"Can I?" Alex cast her moon eyes in his direction.

"Robbie looks like he's been working hard. But, you, kiddo—you look like you've been hardly working."

Alex beamed at Rick. "I've had more practice than Robbie. I'm experienced, so I'm neat."

"You are incredibly cute and persuasive. But you heard what Marquetta said, and she's in charge of the kitchen."

"Did I get a promotion?" Marquetta arched her eyebrows and smiled.

"How long have you worked here?"

"I started part-time when I was in high school."

"And how many years has that been?"

Marquetta laughed and shook her head. "Oh, no. Not so fast, mister. If you want to know my age, you'll have to look it up."

He had. And rather than buoying his spirits, Marquetta's cheerful response gave him another reason to be angry with himself—and his grandfather. She'd only been, what—eighteen— when Captain Jack had sent her off to that fancy San Francisco cooking school? Why had he paid for her education? Just like the story about Marquetta's father, there had to be more than he knew behind the decision. Maybe her father's death and the cooking school were somehow linked. Again, he was the odd man out, but he would not pry.

"When I first got here, you taught me so much about how this place ran," Rick said. "You've steadily taken on more responsibility. And you never complain. You're practically running the B&B. How do you do it?"

She sighed and reached out to touch his arm. "Oh, Rick, I love what I do." She gazed at Alex and smiled as she faced him. "Money isn't everything."

The timer dinged and Alex hopped off the stool. Robbie watched from his seat as Alex and Marquetta raced to the oven. They each donned a pair of mitts. Alex's were a brightly colored children's size Marquetta had given her at Christmas. Marquetta pulled one cookie sheet, Alex took the other. Pressure built behind Rick's eyes as they slid cookies off the hot trays and onto cooling racks. Why couldn't Alex's mother have been more like that?

Marquetta slipped her spatula under the last cookie, looked at Rick, and winked. "No, you can't."

He blinked back tears. Took a deep breath. "Sorry?"

"No, you cannot sample one of my almost famous Seaside Cove Chocolate Chip Cookies, Richard Atwood."

Sweet, perfectly browned, and dotted with melted chips. Oh, man, those babies were divine—especially right out of the oven. "Right. I shouldn't spoil my lunch." He had to admit, even his mouth watered at the thought. "Tell you what, after lunch you kids can each have one. Right now, I have to run into town and talk to Howie Dockham."

He saw concern cross Marquetta's face, but he rushed out of the kitchen before she could ask why he was going to see Howie. As he passed through the dining room, he acknowledged Deputy Cunningham and Hayden. The deputy was writing furiously while Hayden appeared to be somewhat queasy.

At the front desk, Rick dialed the number for Reese's room. When she answered, he asked, "Are you busy?"

"What did you have in mind?"

"Meet me on the front porch. I'd like to take you into town to meet an expert on old documents. Bring your section of the map. And your invitation." He hung up before she could say no.

26

RICK

Rick waited on the front porch for Reese. He spent the time pacing and wondering what he expected to accomplish by asking her to go with him. He could just as easily have asked Monica or one of the others to do this. Why Reese? Honestly, he didn't know.

"Hey, you sure are deep in thought."

And there she was, standing before him. Tan sweater. Skinny jeans. Heels. Dark eyeliner accented her blue eyes. It was a look that came straight out of a fashion shoot. Clearly this wasn't just a trip to meet an old stamp collector like Howie Dockham.

"Stunning," he murmured.

She smiled and looked down at what she wore. "Thanks."

He felt his cheeks grow warm and cleared his throat. "You brought the map?"

She hoisted the purse she'd slung over her shoulder. "In here."

"And the invitation?"

Another nod.

"You sure you'll be okay in those heels? It's about a ten-minute walk."

"Are we going to see some document expert, or did you just want to criticize my wardrobe?"

"Sorry." He turned, descended the stairs, and spoke over his shoulder. "Hope you can keep up."

The clacking of high heels grew louder until Reese strode next to Rick. She cocked one eyebrow in a way that made him want to apologize for having walked away so quickly.

"You're not a very trusting man, are you?"

"I'm working on it. There are people I thought I could trust, but—what am I doing? I'm whining. Nobody likes a whiner." He took the left onto Main Street, surprised she was keeping up so easily. What did he care? She was merely another guest. An attractive one, but as the saying went, they were two ships passing.

Howie's Collectibles was located one store down from the southwest corner of Whale Avenue and Main Street. Like many of the other stores in town, this was an old home long ago converted to business use. Now painted a bright yellow with red and purple trim, Howie's might have stood out in a less colorful town, but this was Seaside Cove, where gaudy was just part of the ambience.

When Rick held the door open for Reese, she narrowed her gaze at him. "Are you kidding me? An antique dealer? I thought we were going to see a document expert."

"He is."

Rick gestured for Reese to enter with a tilt of his head. As she passed, her eyes locked onto his. A hint of floral perfume hung in the air. She brushed away a lock of hair.

"You do that a lot, don't you?" Rick said.

The heels brought her almost to eye level. Inches away. She whispered, "Do what?"

"Push your hair back." His heart hammered in his chest.

"Observant, aren't you?" She licked her lips.

Good God, what was he doing? He had a daughter. A business to run. With a hard swallow, he said, "It's cute."

She gave him a lopsided grin and mouthed, "Oh."

When she slipped away, he allowed himself a moment to breathe a final wisp of perfume. Not until she glanced at him over her shoulder and tilted her head toward the back of the store did he step inside.

The interior of Howie's was a jungle of antiques ranging from large to small. Display cases containing coins and stamps filled the store. Barely a nook or cranny had been left open.

Reese seemed to have little interest in the store inventory, but wended her way through the maze to a counter where a man sat in a wheelchair. Rick recognized him immediately.

They introduced themselves and Howie explained that Joe Gray had already informed him Rick might be coming. Howie asked to see the map. Reese agreed, pulled it from her purse, and smoothed it out on the countertop. Howie donned a pair of white cotton gloves before handling it.

"A precaution." He pulled down the jeweler's loupe affixed to his glasses and inspected the scrap of paper. "Well, well. Good calligraphy, quill pen. That bodes well." He spent another minute examining the map section, then raised the loupe and peered at Reese. "How old did you say this was?"

"Sixteenth century."

"At first glance, it appears that it could be. Paper's no longer white—like it's stained in some way. It has an odd odor I can't place. There's a chance it's genuine, or the paper may have been aged artificially."

"Can you tell?" Rick asked.

Howie shook his head. "We'd have to send it off for testing. You can stain paper in any number of ways to make it appear older than it is. Would you allow me to send it to a friend of mine? He has a lab and is quite meticulous. I can assure you he'll do no damage."

Reese shook her head. "Absolutely no way. I can't take a chance. I'm not letting this out of my sight. "

"You could make a copy of it," Rick said.

She shook her head.

"Young lady," Howie said, "Joe Gray has told me how skeptical he is about this *San Manuel* treasure. Also, you've been carrying this around in your purse as though it were spare change. There's something quite unusual going on here. Aren't you interested in learning the truth about this piece of paper?"

"I am, but there are other ways to handle it," Reese said. "Even if it's not sixteenth century, my gut tells me it's old."

"With one possible exception." Howie lowered the jeweler's loupe and rubbed his gloved finger over the paper. "This is machine-made. The process was unknown prior to the nineteenth century."

Rick shot a glance at Reese, who smiled politely and pocketed the scrap. What was she pulling? Howie was right. Reese hadn't treated the map like it was five-hundred years old. Nor was she being rational about checking its legitimacy. For that matter, he'd seen tourists be more careful with their Seaside Cove Visitor Maps.

"Nineteenth century is still pretty old," Reese said. "I'm hopeful."

Howie returned her smile and shrugged. "If it turns out to be legitimate, the stains would make sense."

"Thank you for your help, Howie." Rick glanced at Reese. It was his turn to raise an eyebrow.

She murmured her appreciation, but seemed anxious to leave. As they walked out, Rick glanced back into the shop. Howie grimaced and shook his head. Rick understood. He wanted to throw his hands up in the air and scream in frustration. If the map wasn't from the sixteenth century, how old was it? When and why had it been created? And did she already know the answers to those questions?

27

RICK

Rick took his time closing the door to Howie's Collectibles. He had so many questions running through his head, but he felt sure Reese wasn't yet ready to trust him with the answers. When he turned away from the store, she was standing in front of the Crooked Mast.

"You said their food is good?" She cocked her head and peered into the front window of the restaurant.

"The locals love it."

The Crooked Mast drew a hefty lunch and dinner crowd. It was another of Seaside Cove's gaudy attractions with green siding, orange trim, and white accents. This was one of those times Rick was thankful Captain Jack had stuck to basic white for the B&B.

"They don't open for another half hour," Rick said.

"I see the hours posted." She closed the distance between them. Let her gaze rest on his. "Look, I appreciate you trying to help. But, you have to understand, this is a complex issue. The map may be a fake. The *San Manuel* is real. Period. Who's this guy Joe Gray that Howie mentioned?"

"He runs Gray's Sailing Charters. He's done a lot of work with treasure hunters in the past."

She turned away and again examined the restaurant. A few seconds later, she looked at him and smiled. "Can he get me a boat?"

Thank goodness the ruse he'd used earlier with Joe might actually turn out to be true. However, something wasn't right in the way she was acting. She was either the biggest flirt he'd ever seen, or she was deliberately trying to keep him off balance. Rick took a small step toward her. "Well, sure. You want to talk to him?"

"Lead the way."

They walked in silence to the wharf. There were so many things Rick didn't understand about this woman or her friends. They followed the ramp to the boats, bypassed a large yacht, and stopped at Joe Gray's houseboat.

"Ah, you're back," Joe said as he looked up from the small wooden cabinet he'd been sanding on the front deck. "Come aboard."

"Thanks," Rick said. "This is Reese, one of the people I mentioned."

Joe placed the sandpaper in a small plastic toolkit, wiped his hands on his jeans, and groaned as he stood. "Nice to meet you, Miss..."

"Potok, Reese Potok," she said as she shook his hand.

"Glad you came. I'm happy to have a break from maintenance. It's a constant battle against the elements with this old girl. Sometimes I wonder why I don't get myself a little apartment so I don't have to fight this never-ending battle. The problem is, I love being on the water. I wouldn't want to be anywhere else."

Reese gave Joe a warm smile, then eyed the boat. "She's a beauty. Is that all teak paneling on the sides?"

"Yup. They don't make them like this anymore. She's solid through-and-through." He ran his fingers over the wood. "Everything today is fiberglass this and composite that." He pointed in the general direction of the B&B. "This boat is a lot like that place of yours, Rick. A grand old lady. She needs to be taken care of, but she'll survive the years with proper maintenance."

"We're trying to get her there," Rick said.

"Captain Jack and his big remodel." Joe turned back to Reese. "I assume you want that boat Rick mentioned earlier."

"Yes. Something with a dive platform and good speed. My team has a spot we'd like to investigate off the coast."

"Your team?" Rick gaped at her. "I thought none of you liked each other? You're really going to work with the other treasure hunters?"

She gave him a confident smile. "Under the right circumstances." She cocked an eyebrow at Joe. "Well?"

"You do realize there is, in all likelihood, no Spanish gold out there. The gold traveled either to Manila for trade or back to Spain. And it's highly improbable that, as your group seems to believe, a hurricane blew a ship this far north."

"Mr. Gray...Joe, I realize you probably think because I'm a woman I don't know what I'm talking about. But, I've been researching the *San Manuel* for years, and I know Spanish ships left Acapulco bound for the Philippines loaded with silver. When they returned, they carried porcelain, spices, and silks. There are a number of ships unaccounted for—like the *Content*, for instance. The fact is, no matter what the *San Manuel* contains, what matters to me is being the one to find her. So, are you going to charter a boat for me or not? I've only got a day or two left and I need to test my theory."

Joe raised his eyebrows and nodded at Reese. "Little lady, you've got yourself a boat—as long as I'm the captain."

28

ALEX

Daddy just left with Miss Potok. She's all dressed up. Kinda like my mom dressed. She stood real close to him. Flipped her hair back. And the way she was watching him. I might only be a kid, but I can tell when a girl is flirting. I can't believe he abandoned us...for her.

I jump when Marquetta comes up behind me. She kneels next to me and puts her hands on my shoulders. I lean into her as hot tears well up from deep inside.

"I'm so sorry, Alex. I thought you might get some time with your dad."

"It's not fair!" My voice cracks and the first tear dribbles down my cheek. "Why's he like her?"

"Who, Sweetie?"

"Miss Potok! She met Daddy, and they left together. I saw them. I saw them!"

Marquetta's got a frown on her face and I'm sure she's sad, too. She doesn't like Miss Potok either. She doesn't wipe away my tears, but pulls me in close and hugs me again. This time I don't let go, but hang on. It feels good. Like something from long ago...

"Sweetie, you can't be spying on your dad. It's not right."

"But they were acting like...like they were going on a date."

Marquetta's jaw is kinda pinched and her eyes are all watery. "It doesn't matter. We can't control who other people like." She sniffles and clears her throat. "Come on. I have work to do."

She stands up and smiles at me. I can tell she's faking it. She hurts, too.

"You and Robbie did a good job with the cookies. Why don't you go upstairs and play?"

"Okay."

Robbie's been standing at the butler door trying to ignore what's going on. But he asked that question when we were in Miss Kelley's room, and Marquetta will have the answer. "What's unequivi-cable mean?"

"Where'd you hear that, Sweetie?"

"I read it someplace."

"It helps to have some context. But, it basically means without doubt."

"So, like, undying love?"

"Where's this going, Alex?"

I glance over at Robbie. He's been through a lot. I totally don't want to be crying in front of him. But I'm glad he was here even though he looks like he wants to be somewhere else.

"Just curious. C'mon, Robbie."

I grab his hand, and he follows me up the stairs. We're at the top and Marquetta is still standing in the lobby. She's sniffling and looks lonely. I want to go to her, but she turns away and heads for the kitchen before I make up my mind.

"Robbie, Marquetta's gonna be busy and my dad's gone. You know what that means?"

He shakes his head. I roll my eyes. Wanna say something about boys being clueless, but there are two men down the hall whispering and I don't want them to hear us. When I look, I see it's Mr. Joshua and Mr. Luhan. Together? They're angry, too. I close my eyes and listen, but it's hard to make out what they're saying. After a few seconds, I pull Robbie in the other direction.

"Where we going, Alex?" Robbie's eyes are real big cause he's staring down at the master key in my hand. "Are we spying again?"

"We're gonna check out the Fore Sail Room. That's where Miss Potok is staying."

He grins at me. "Awesome."

Getting in is easy, just like before. We close the door, and I look around. It's kinda disappointing cause she's picked up. "This sucks. She's another neat freak." I take in a deep breath cause I'm determined to find something. "Look under the bed."

Robbie gets on his knees and does what I asked while I start going through the dresser drawers. There's nothing. No diary. No papers. Nothing.

The room is getting blurry again. I can't have been wrong about Miss Potok. I can't! I want to slam my fist into something!

"Alex?"

"What?" I sniffle.

"I think you're gonna want to see this."

"Okay." I take a deep breath. Get ready for another huge disappointment. I swipe away a tear and turn around.

My jaw drops.

Robbie spreads a huge piece of paper out on top of the bed. We both stand there looking down at it.

"Holy crap, Robbie. This is a totally different treasure map."

29

RICK

The meeting with Joe Gray ended with Reese agreeing to Joe's terms. They scheduled a departure time of first light the following morning. Joe would captain the vessel. With the deal made, Rick thought about asking Reese to lunch. Was it because he felt an attraction? Or was he keeping his enemies close?

He asked. She declined. More business to handle in town. Which raised another question—what other business could she possibly have in Seaside Cove?

Questions nagged at him during the walk home. He arrived to find Alex, Marquetta, and Robbie on the back patio. They were laughing. Smiling. Happy. A welcome relief, actually.

"Hey, what's going on?" Rick asked.

"Marquetta wanted to eat out here, Daddy. Are you gonna have lunch with us?"

Rick glanced at Marquetta.

She averted her eyes before she stood and gave him a polite smile. "I have plenty of salad makings. Have a seat; it'll only take a sec."

He sat. Marquetta stood and went into the kitchen. Rick chitchatted with the kids, but couldn't stop from glancing over his shoulder. Two women. So different. And confusing.

When Marquetta returned, he stared at the plate in front of him. "Wow, salad heaven. Tomato, carrots, and some leftover chicken. Nice and healthy."

"I can get you something else if you'd prefer," she said.

"Nope, this is good." He winked at her, got no response. Maybe he could lighten the mood? He pretended to eye Alex's and Robbie's plates. "PB&J with potato chips. It pays to be a kid around here."

"Would you prefer a sandwich?" Marquetta snapped.

Rick raised both hands. "No, I was just kidding. A salad's great. So what's been going on?" And what had he done to irritate Marquetta so much? He'd never seen her like this.

Robbie picked at his chips, but Alex ignored her food.

"Daddy, where did you go with Miss Potok?"

"Ah, long story, kiddo. The short one is we wanted to see Howie Dockham. What did you do while I was gone?"

"I'd like to know that, too," Marquetta said. "When I looked for them earlier, they were nowhere to be found."

"We were playing hide-and-seek," Alex said. "You didn't find us."

Her ear-to-ear grin was a little over-the-top as far as Rick was concerned. He crossed his arms. "Really."

"Sounds suspicious to me." Marquetta frowned as she glanced at Alex.

"So what did Mr. Dockham say?" Alex immediately bit into her sandwich.

It was obvious she was working hard to divert attention from what she and Robbie had been up to. He might pursue that line of inquiry if Robbie weren't here, but those questions had to wait for now.

"Howie inspected the map we showed him. He believes it's fake and wanted to send it off for testing, but Reese declined. He said the paper seemed too new. It had an odd odor to it."

"Wait." Marquetta said with her fork poised in midair. "What kind of odor?"

All eyes focused on Rick. The only sounds were those of the distant ocean surf and the kids munching on their chips. Rick shrugged. "Howie said he couldn't place it."

"Was it a floral aroma?" Marquetta stabbed a cherry tomato and popped it in her mouth.

"It didn't smell like any flower I recognize."

"Was it a love note?" Robbie gazed at Rick and Marquetta with wide eyes.

Alex clamped her hand over her mouth and coughed, then reached for her milk. She took several gulps as Rick watched her.

"No Robbie," Rick said. "It wasn't a love note. Are you okay, kiddo?"

The girl nodded and took another swallow.

"Then why did it smell like flowers?" Robbie asked.

"I've got the same question." Rick gave the boy a thumbs up, then watched Alex closely.

"Miss Kelley was in her room when I popped in with fresh linens," Marquetta said. "She showed me her section of the map. It had a very distinct odor."

"That's exactly what Howie said." Rick shook his head. "But he couldn't identify it."

"It's Darjeeling oolong tea." Marquetta shrugged and held his gaze.

"It's what?" Rick screwed up his face to show his skepticism. "How would you know that?"

"I studied teas in cooking school. Just as aroma is important in wine tasting, it also plays a role in teas. Her part of the map reminded me of a divine oolong tea from China."

Rick listened to the rhythm of the surf slapping the shore. He raised an eyebrow and looked at Marquetta. "Are you positive?"

Marquetta straightened up in her chair; her jaw tightened. "I know my teas, Rick."

"Sorry. I didn't mean to sound like I doubted you. I had no idea you were a tea expert."

She leaned back, closed her eyes, and took a measured breath. "It's okay. What I smelled was a second flush Darjeeling oolong. It has a very rare muscatel flavor and is quite expensive."

"What's that mean?" Alex asked.

Rick rubbed the back of his neck and cleared his throat. "That this whole *San Manuel* thing is a fake."

"It is," Alex blurted.

Rick sighed. And what did that mean? He stared at Alex, but she was avoiding eye contact. How could she be so positive? Because she was a kid? Or she knew something. He turned to Marquetta. "You said your father was into chasing treasure."

She closed her eyes and paused. "Yes."

"I just want to ask you one question. And it's not about him. Have you ever heard of the *San Manuel*?"

"No. This one's all new to me."

"That's what Joe said, too. He's certainly been around a while. I guess he worked with your dad at one point."

Marquetta dropped her fork and stared at Rick. "How do you know that?"

He pressed his lips together and swallowed the lump in his throat. "We went there to charter a boat."

To his left, Alex sat watching him. He'd told her so many times how she should be honest. He couldn't lie. Not to Marquetta. The lump settled deep in the pit of his stomach and the words tumbled out.

"When he told me he worked with your father—I shouldn't have asked the questions I did. I'm sorry."

"This happened with Miss Potok there?"

He shook his head and croaked, "Before."

"Before what?" Marquetta glared at him with an anger Rick had never seen before.

"After Devon was here. When breakfast was over, I left and went into town. That was the first time I saw Joe."

The color drained from Marquetta's face. She stood. Held his gaze. "So you lied to me."

"Yes," he whispered.

Tears welled in her eyes. "I trusted you." She stormed away without another word.

Alex jumped up and raced after her. "Marquetta, wait."

Rick's insides twisted. He wanted to follow Marquetta, but his feet were encased in concrete. "Let her go, Alex. She's right. I made a terrible mistake."

"Stop her, Daddy!" Tears streamed down Alex's cheeks and she appeared torn between chasing after Marquetta and coming back to the table.

Rick walked, stiff-legged, to Alex. He put an arm around her shoulder, but she jerked away.

"You've ruined everything!"

"Come sit down," he said. "She's upset with me, not you. Give her some time to cool off." He turned his attention back to Robbie. "And you have company."

"I don't understand, Daddy...why's Marquetta so mad at you?"

"It wasn't right for me to ask questions about her without her permission. She feels like her privacy has been violated. It's why we always notify guests when we need to enter their rooms."

Alex stiffened; Robbie stopped nibbling on his chips and began chewing on his lower lip. What had these two done?

He knelt next to his daughter and held her at arm's length while he kept an eye on Robbie. "You have something to tell me, don't you?"

Alex's thin frame shuddered in his arms. At the table, Robbie couldn't take his eyes from her.

"I promise I won't get angry, but you need to tell me what it is." His voice grew stern as he added the final emphasis. "Right now."

"We were spying," Robbie mumbled.

"Robbie!" Alex stared at the boy with her mouth open.

"Spying?" Rick looked straight into his daughter's eyes. "Alex?"

"We wanted to help you solve Mr. Gordon's murder." She hung her head as if she were talking to the concrete.

"Alex, look at me. You entered a guest's room without permission?"

She nodded; so did Robbie.

Rick's stomach clenched at their confession. He cleared his throat. "What did you do, Alex?"

"We kinda found a note in Miss Kelley's room to Mr. Gordon. It sounded like they were arguing because she was jealous of Miss Potok. Miss Kelley said she wanted to apologize because she was wrong about Mr. Gordon and Miss Potok."

"What I meant was, how did you get in?"

Alex reached into her front pocket and pulled out the master key. Rick recognized it immediately. She handed it over without a word.

Who did he blame for this turn of events? A child who'd made a mistake? Or himself? Better yet, what did he do about it?

30

ALEX

June 17

Hey Journal,

This is like the suckiest day ever. Marquetta's gone home mad and I'm in trouble again. It's all that Miss Potok's fault. She's lying to Daddy about the map and he doesn't get it cause she's always acting sweet with him. I think that's one reason Marquetta went home and now things are bad between all of us.

I don't even care about finding Daddy a girlfriend anymore. I just want Marquetta to be my friend. I totally miss her. What am I gonna do if she doesn't come back? She gave you to me so I could really talk to someone who wouldn't judge me. Now I see how special that is. Please Journal, you gotta help me. There has to be a way to fix this.

Maybe I'll text Marquetta. I hope she's still talking to me.

xoxo

Alex

31

RICK

Sending Alex to her room was easy. Getting Robbie home turned into one of those easier-said-than-done tasks. Robbie's mom and dad were both in town for a medical appointment. Marquetta was still AWOL. And Rick was in no mood to serve as Robbie's babysitter. As a last resort, he called Deputy Cunningham on his meter reading route. Adam agreed to stop by, collect Robbie, and drive him into town. He also promised to come back after he read the last meter.

Rick opened the door to his office and eyed the visitor's wingback chair in front of his desk. Captain Jack had called it the hot seat. He smiled at the memory. Captain Jack had also told him this room had a calming effect. "It's like an old library. There's patience. Knowledge. Truth."

So many things didn't make sense. A murder. How he'd gone behind Marquetta's back. And Alex—sneaking around the B&B. Rick entered the room and sat in the hot seat. He stared at his chair. The one he'd inherited from his grandfather and imagined him, craggy face and all, watching with those hard brown eyes from the chair behind the desk.

"What about it, Captain Jack? Are you going to give me some grand words of wisdom?"

Silence. Rick drank in the smell of leather and old books.

"I didn't think so," he said.

The mute presence dared him to continue. Dig deeper. Stop hiding.

"Everything's closing in around me, Captain Jack. I'm losing my daughter. This murder investigation is a spiderweb of deceit and lies. And I might have destroyed the trust of someone I really care about."

He leaned back. Stretched his legs.

"You always told me to solve the biggest problem first. Well, that's Gordon's murder. And Alex is right, Deputy Cunningham is a nice guy, but he can't do it alone."

Rick stood, took a deep breath, and loosened his shoulders.

"Get out of my chair, old man. You left me this place, and that murder is a black stain on our reputation. On mine. I won't let my daughter see me as a failure. Marquetta, either. I don't know what's up with her, but you've got something to do with it. Someday, I'll figure it out. Until then, I've got a murder to solve."

The overstuffed leather monstrosity whooshed as Rick sat and fired up his computer. His pulse quickened. His breathing grew shallow. Somewhere in here were one or more clues. His job was to find them.

He began with the images of the body. Photo number eight clearly showed Gordon sprawled over the rocks face down. Rick zoomed in. Gordon's wet clothing clung like moss on a rock. Rick closed his eyes, imagined the feel of it, heavy with moisture, but not dripping wet, either.

Patience. Knowledge. Truth.

What a joke. There had been so little of those recently around the Seaside Cove B&B. Time for more. Rick examined the same photo again. This time, it seemed more complete. He saw more detail.

Gordon's death was like an onion waiting to be peeled back one layer at a time. This photo might be in the first layer, or the tenth.

"Do what you did in New York. Dig deeper," he said. "Find the facts."

So what were the facts? The real ones. Not something a treasure hunter concocted.

First, he knew he'd caught Cadman retrieving the monopod from the rocks. Which meant it should be in these photos. It wasn't. Nor had Deputy Cunningham's search turned it up. Nowhere in any of these photos were there any signs of a monopod. Nothing.

He stood and went to the window. In the distance, the shoreline beckoned. So many cracks and crevices in those rocks. Exactly which one had hidden the monopod? Rick glanced back at the photo on his laptop.

"How did you know exactly where that thing was, Cadman?"

Yes. That was one question. No more vague BS like a little birdie told him. He turned back to the ocean and watched the swells roll toward land, gradually build to a high crest and deep trough, then roar in.

He hurried back to his desk and slid his fingers over the trackpad of his Mac until he brought up photo number twelve. It and eight were the best "body" shots. Arms crossed, he reclined in his chair and tilted his head to one side as he tried to visualize what might have happened before he arrived. He scrolled forward through photos until he got to the ones of the paramedics. The scene was as he remembered it. Two big guys had Gordon's body on a lightweight carrier. Even in the photo, they obviously struggled to keep their balance. Just like Cadman last night.

Rick scrolled back to photo number twelve. Marquetta had said the guests were pawing over the body. But, Gordon lay face down. Anyone trying to find something like a map would have wanted to check Gordon's front pockets as well as his back. When he and Adam had inventoried the scene, their working theory had been someone turned the body over. In retrospect, that couldn't have happened.

The rocks were too uneven. Too jagged. A mountain goat might be surefooted out there, but not a person. With all the deep crevices and sharp angles, walking down there was treacherous even for young, big guys like those paramedics. Rick had the photo to prove it. The bottom line was good old gravity made it physically impossible for any of these people to have rolled the body for a thorough search.

But what about photo number eight? The wet clothing? He scrolled back-and-forth between eight and his one ocean shot. He'd caught the current surging out. The ocean surface was a good two feet below the rock he'd been standing on. And the rock was nearly dry. So if the body had been found on a boulder a few feet in from where he took that photo, and if those rocks were otherwise dry, Gordon must have been in the ocean. And he didn't get out on his own.

Now he had three big questions. Was the *San Manuel* real? Who had the missing map section? And who had helped Gordon climb out of the ocean?

Rick looked at the wall where an old map of the bay outside Seaside Cove hung. Many years ago, Captain Jack had the map framed under protective glass. It seemed kind of silly, actually, because it was just part of a USGS topographical map. Rick rested his finger on the glass over a spot in the middle of the bay. Cadman called Gordon's the "X marks the spot" section. And his guests all wanted it. Even if they found it, what would they do with it?

In fact, who were these people? Other than liars. How were they tied together? Other than their little treasure hunting club. Rick returned to his chair and opened the computer program containing their guest registrations.

After doing a nearly worthless background check on each of them, he had nothing new. Hayden Kalstone and Heath Santiago were from different parts of Los Angeles; Cadman Richardson listed his address as Huntington Park; Bradford Luhan, Glendale;

and Mark Joshua, Rosemead. These guys were, literally, all over the map.

Just to be thorough, he also checked the registrations for Reese and Monica. They were from San Clemente and Lakewood, respectively. He recognized Monica's address from the envelope she'd shown him at breakfast.

The return address was Gordon's. But, what if someone faked the invitations? They would have also faked the return address. He pulled an envelope from today's mail out of his inbox. Whoever sent those invitations knew the addresses of the others. Easy to find in a group like this. They certainly would have known Gordon's address. What they couldn't fake, though, was the postmark.

And Monica had an envelope with just that. At last, had he found the truth? If Gordon didn't send the invitations—if the weekend really was a setup—things changed.

Drastically.

It made Gordon's death premeditated murder.

32

ALEX

I told Daddy last night how much I love my room. It totally has all my favorite colors. This is the prettiest girl's room ever. And it was fun working with Marquetta to decorate. She did an awesome job. She knew exactly what I wanted. And now I might never see her again.

She's not talking to me. She didn't answer my text.

Daddy always tells me things will get better with time. I don't understand why grownups say that. Do they think it's gonna make us kids feel better? My dad still misses my mom. He's super sad a lot and won't ever talk about her.

Now that Daddy and Marquetta had that big fight she's never gonna come back and I don't wanna hurt anymore. It totally sucks not being able to have the one thing I want more than anything.

There's a knock on my door. It's probably Daddy. I don't want to see him right now. He's the one who made Marquetta mad. "Go away."

"Alex? Sweetie? Would you open the door?"

"Marquetta?"

I scramble off the bed and unlock the door. When I open it, she's standing in front of me. All blurry through my tears. I reach out. She steps forward. Oh my God, she feels good.

"You're here. You're really here."

"Oh, Sweetie."

She hugs me back and I never want this feeling to end.

"Can I come in?"

I feel my head nodding, but I can't talk. My throat's all tight and my eyes are totally burning.

"Let's sit down. Okay?"

I keep my arms wrapped around her as she leads me to the bed. If I let go, she might leave again. When we sit on the bed, she hugs me. I snuggle closer and just want to be quiet and feel her arm around me.

Marquetta's so strong. She's become, like, my idol. Or my mom. When I can finally talk, I sniffle, "Marquetta, aren't you afraid of anything?"

She brushes the hair away from my face and kisses my forehead. "Everybody has something that scares them, Sweetie."

"But you never get scared and you don't let stuff bother you. You got mad, but you came back."

"I'm not leaving you. How could I?" She smiles at me and presses my cheek with her fingertips to wipe away a tear. "You've got enough worries. Growing up is a hard job. I understand how difficult it is. I had plenty of drama when I was your age."

Her touch totally comforts me. "Like what?"

"Oh, boys, school, the usual. The same kinds of problems you're facing now. If you need someone to talk to, I'm here."

I curl up in her lap. The way she cradles me makes the pain fade away.

"Everybody's mad at me."

"That's a heavy load, Sweetie—everybody. Like who? Robbie?"

"He's mad cause I got him in trouble. Is he ever gonna talk to me again?"

"I'm sure he will."

"He never says anything about what happened to his mom. Do you know?"

"It's not a secret, Alex. Robbie's dad worked for a big company. Robbie's mom was an elementary school teacher. They were on vacation when she was injured in an auto accident. Robbie and his dad only had minor injuries, but his mom was in the hospital for a long time. Robbie's dad had to quit his job so he could stay home and take care of her and Robbie. These days, life's a constant struggle for them."

"Could we do something to help them?"

"I tell you what, why don't you come up with an idea? We'll work on it together. You like Robbie, don't you, Sweetie?"

"Yeah. A lot."

"I hope you understand Robbie's not the last boy you'll like. There was a time when I cried myself to sleep for months because a boy looked at me the wrong way. At that moment, I thought it was the end of the world. I hated my mom because she told me there would be others, but eventually I realized she was right. There were other boys. If Robbie doesn't get over this, then it wasn't meant to be."

I sit up and look at Marquetta. "Are you alone because you never found one that was meant to be?"

Her jaw gets all puckery. She looks out the window and chews on her lower lip. "I don't know, Alex. I hoped there might be one, but now I'm not so sure."

"Is it Daddy?"

She strokes my shoulder with her hand. "Whatever happens between your dad and me will never change how I feel about you. And you'll come to realize if you make a mistake, it doesn't mean your dad will love you any less."

"Even if I don't like his new girlfriend?"

Marquetta sits back like someone slapped her. "Why do you think he has a girlfriend?"

"Cause he's spending so much time with Miss Potok."

"Sweetie, that doesn't mean they're involved romantically. Besides, she'll be leaving soon."

"And then we can go back to the way it was before she got here?"

But she doesn't say what I want to hear. She looks really sad. Like I feel right now.

"Things have changed, Alex. Your dad violated my trust."

"But I did the same thing. I violated Daddy's trust, and you said he'd forgive me. Why can't you forgive him?"

It takes forever and my heart is pounding while I wait for her to tell me everything will be okay. I bury my face in her T-shirt. "All I want is for things to be the way they were before."

"We can't really go back, Sweetie. I wish we could. How did you violate your dad's trust?"

We sit there holding onto each other for a long time. Marquetta seems to know I need her touch right now. The longer she holds me, the stronger I get until finally the words just come out. "Me and Robbie kinda broke into Miss Kelley's room."

"Oh, I see."

She's totally gonna leave. I just know it. But she doesn't. "You're not mad?"

"You made a mistake, Alex. We all do." She kinda laughs to herself. "At least you didn't take a ride in the dumbwaiter."

"What we use for the laundry?"

Marquetta bites her lip and says, "It's no longer safe. The equipment is very old."

"You totally rode it!"

She pushes me away and looks into my eyes. "You have to promise me you won't get inside. Your dad would never forgive me for telling you this."

"Was it scary?"

Marquetta grips my shoulders and frowns. "It's off limits, Alex. Got it? Just like Miss Kelley's room. That's why your dad wants you to stay up here. You have to think about what you've done and understand it was wrong."

"But me and Robbie were trying to help Daddy investigate."

"I'm sure you wanted to help, but you made a bad decision."

"I tried to explain why we did it, but Daddy was too mad. He didn't even care when I told him about the note we found. Miss Kelley was trying to make up with Mr. Gordon."

Marquetta huffs. She sounds frustrated. "You understand why sneaking into her room was wrong, don't you?"

"Yes. It's that trust thing. I get it, but if I'm gonna be in jail, somebody ought to know what else we found out."

"Oh, Sweetie." She sounds super disappointed. "Is that your way of telling me you broke into another guest's room?"

"Mr. Santiago's."

"Oh, Lordy."

I can tell she's mad, but she can't stop herself from smiling at me.

Then, she says, "All right. You can confess. What did you find out?"

"He had all sorts of news stories about Mr. Gordon. It's kinda like one of those stalkers."

"What an age we live in." Marquetta shakes her head and grips my shoulders tighter.

I frown and look up at her. "How come you're so upset?"

"The fact that a ten-year-old knows about stalkers troubles me deeply. So that's it? All you found were news stories?"

"They went back a few years. I read a couple of them. There must have been a lot of money involved."

"Money? Why do you say that?"

"Because they were all about treasure hunts."

Marquetta nods to herself. "Is there anything else? Please tell me you didn't go into any other rooms."

I wanna tell her about Miss Potok and the map, but the way she said that has me worried I'll disappoint her and so I can't tell her. I so wish I could, but instead I shake my head. "No."

"Thank goodness. I need to have a talk with your dad. I'll see if I can't get you out of jail."

I hug her again. "It's not so bad now. You're here."

Marquetta waits until I pull back. When she stands up and looks down at me, she looks super sad again. She's blinking back tears and I know I have to tell her. I have to. I'm gonna burst if I don't so I throw my arms around her again. It feels so good. Just like...

"I love you, Marquetta."

She makes a funny little noise. Then she kisses my forehead. "I love you, too, Sweetie."

33

RICK

Rick sat behind his desk, reclining in the plush leather chair that had once been Captain Jack's. He couldn't avert his eyes from the top left drawer of the desk.

The key to why he was so down lay inside.

It symbolized so much, and so little.

He slid the drawer open.

Inside, there were a few pens and pencils, a stapler, and a box of paperclips. And next to those, it lay.

He swallowed hard and picked up the three-inch strand of bright red yarn.

His cheeks burned with the memory as he held it. It was the first thing she'd given him.

She'd tied it around his finger on his second day when he'd forgotten to refill the upstairs coffee carafes. Marquetta probably thought he'd thrown it out or lost it long ago. But, for some silly reason, he hadn't. He'd placed that little piece of yarn in his drawer for safekeeping. Each day he saw it—and her. Leaning in close. Tying the ends into a bow. Smiling at him in a way that captured his heart.

He couldn't imagine throwing it, or her, away.

A gentle knock jarred the vision from his thoughts. Rick put the yarn back in its place and cleared his throat. "Yes?"

Slowly, the door opened and a white handkerchief appeared. He recognized the hand holding it immediately.

"Come in," he said softly.

Marquetta stuck her head through the opening. "I came to apologize for blowing up at you."

"No." Rick raised both hands. "You had every right. I was in the wrong."

"Truce?"

"Happily," he whispered. He gestured at the chair in front of his desk.

Marquetta winced. "I haven't sat in the hot seat since Captain Jack told me he was dying."

Rick sucked in a breath and waited while she eased the door shut and slowly made her way to the chair. They remained silent—he, determined not to pry; she, apparently not yet ready to abandon her secrets.

Marquetta shrugged and let her gaze flit around the room before returning to Rick's. "He always told me if I had to sit here it was going to be really bad news."

Rick shook his head. "No more bad news today. I couldn't handle it. Have you seen Alex?"

"She's the reason I'm here."

His muscles tensed. He glanced at the drawer with the yarn stored safely inside. Of course. Alex. Over the course of their time here, he'd encouraged their relationship. Lately, he feared what might happen if he drove Marquetta away. "I see," he said.

"She told me she'd been given a time out."

The pressure behind his eyes built, and he struggled to sound curious instead of offended. He took a last look at the top left drawer before asking, "Did she tell you why?"

"She did."

"Do you think I was wrong?"

"Not at all. In fact, I reinforced that she'd made a mistake. But, I did ask her what she learned."

Rick recalled his reaction when Alex had confessed. He ran a hand through his hair and sighed. "I kind of lost it when I found out what she'd done."

"I don't blame you. Something like that might bring on serious repercussions. Nevertheless, you need to know what she discovered since you're helping Adam. You are still working with him, right?"

Marquetta leaned forward, obviously waiting. He nodded.

"Good," she said. "Alex found a note from Miss Kelley to Mr. Gordon. She thinks they were getting back together. Quite possibly, it's no more than a young girl romanticizing things, but..." She let the word hang in the air.

"Alex told me about the note."

"But, I don't think she said anything about Mr. Santiago."

His stomach did a flip flop. "I'm afraid we didn't get beyond Miss Kelley. What did she do to him?"

"She found what sounds like a collection of news stories about him and Mr. Gordon. From the way Alex described it, he might have been jealous." Marquetta shrugged. She eased herself forward as though preparing to leave. "I wanted you to know."

"Don't go yet," he blurted, then bit his lower lip. "That came out wrong," he stammered. "What I meant was, I'd like to make it up to you."

Marquetta's gray eyes misted over and she swallowed hard. She glanced from side-to-side, then swiped at her cheek with her fingers. "All I've ever asked is to be respected. That includes my privacy."

Cold permeated every bone in Rick's body. What had he expected? *I love you. I want to be part of your life.* No, that was the stuff of a child's fantasies. Alex might expect it to happen, but he felt—no, knew—deep down, it was too much to ask. He took in a short breath and nodded.

"You've got it." A moment later, he said, "Can I ask for your impression of what Alex told you?"

She seemed to ponder the question for a few seconds. "I didn't see these news stories, so I'm not sure if she got it right. What I have seen is the way Monica glares at Reese all the time. Have you noticed?"

"All the time? Is that one of those generalities like it's always foggy in California?" Rick laughed, but stopped when Marquetta gave him a blank stare. "You're serious," he said.

"It's not constant. But, there's a definite animosity between those two women. I overheard Miss Kelley on the phone with someone—it sounded like a girlfriend. She was really catty about Miss Potok. She kept going on about how this woman was trying to steal her boyfriend away from her. Miss Kelley strikes me as codependent. She's very needy, so maybe that's why she wrote the note. It might have been a last ditch effort to get him back."

"Huh. Reese did say Monica wanted to settle down and have a family."

"Do you suppose Miss Kelley had reason to suspect Miss Potok was attempting to take away her future husband?"

"You know what? I need to find out. I'll talk to her."

"Miss Potok?"

"No, Monica. I'm beginning to suspect the relationship between Reese and Gordon was more than casual."

34

RICK

Rick found Monica down by the water. She stood on the paved walkway, well back from the surging waves, the sea spray, and the murder location. Even from a distance, he could see the mascara-stained tracks left by her tears.

"Hey, Monica."

She flinched and faced him, then wiped her cheeks with the palms of her hands, leaving behind black patches of skin. "Why'd it happen?"

"That's what I'm trying to find out. I need your help."

"How would I do that? I'm not an investigator."

"You might have information."

"Such as?"

"You said you were close to Jim. Were you engaged?"

"He was going to propose. It just hadn't happened yet."

"Why not?"

"Because we had a fight." She glared in the direction of the B&B. "I found out he'd been sleeping with Reese. He said it meant nothing—how cliché. Isn't that what men always say?"

Rick paused and considered the parallels to his own disastrous marriage. "I suppose. So that's why you dislike Reese so much?"

"Yes. Not only because she's a slut, but because she lied about it. I thought we were friends. You'd think she would have had the guts to tell me to my face, but I had to hear about it from Brad."

"What did he tell you?"

"That they were having an affair. A liaison, as he called it."

"How'd he find out they were involved?"

She snuck another glance at the B&B. "He's an incurable gossip."

Rick watched the ocean surf roll in for a few seconds. More parallels, he thought. No doubt about it, people liked to talk about other people. When you were the object, it hurt. But, in this case one of the two parties was dead and the other keeping secrets. This was one of those times when being plugged into the rumor mill might be of help. Before he went down that path, he needed to determine how reliable Brad's information was.

"What did he say?"

"He—no—this is too much. I'd prefer to be alone if you don't mind."

Rick sighed, cursed his bad luck, but remained determined to press on. "One or two more questions. That's all. Okay?"

"Whatever."

"You showed me your invitation yesterday at breakfast. Would you let me see it again?"

For a moment, she looked like she might say no, then she shrugged. "I guess. I was looking at it myself last night." Monica reached into her bag and handed Rick the envelope she'd shown him at the table.

"Thanks." He read the return address. "I thought so. This is Jim's, isn't it?"

"Yes."

"But the postmark isn't the same zip code. Did you notice that?"

Another yes.

Rick waited as she wrung her hands while she gazed out to sea. When he shifted his weight to the other foot, she seemed to sense the movement and peered at him.

"That's Cadman's zip code," she said. "I'll bet he set up this entire weekend. Should I turn this over to the police so they can question him again? I wouldn't doubt that he and Reese conspired to murder Jim."

"Why would Cadman and Reese work together? Better yet, why go to all that trouble?" Assembling eight people just to kill one of them seemed beyond ridiculous—maybe even delusional. Perhaps Monica was grasping for any solution no matter how desperate it might be. "Besides, Cadman has a shoulder injury. He's not physically able to lift his arm high enough to wield a weapon."

"Don't kid yourself. You haven't seen him when he's loaded up on oxy. Wouldn't be the first time. That's why he's got such a terrible memory."

"Oxycodone? Are you sure about that?"

Monica stammered. Her gaze darted away and Rick wondered if she'd created a lie she now found too complex to manage. He was convinced all of these people were lying about one thing or another. What was Monica's lie?

Tears trickled down her nose and fell to the pavement as she stared down. Her nod was nothing more than a slight bobbing of her head.

"How do you know he's using drugs?" Rick demanded.

Her fingers flitted to her mouth and came to rest on her neck. "There are signs. Things like he'll be totally relaxed and out of the blue he'll go off into one of these moods. Really bad. He said something once about Brad and his shady background." She hesitated before she continued. "You should be aware that Brad's as crooked as they come. Jim liked him. At least he used to. He said he made a ton of money off Brad's stock tips. Then they had some kind of falling out."

"Brad Luhan is a stock trader? I thought he was an accountant."

"Don't kid yourself," Monica snickered. "Brad's no more of an accountant than you or I. That's just what he tells people. Brad is the CFO of his own life. He's a clerk, that's all. It's true, he works for an accounting firm, but Brad doesn't interface with the firm's clients."

Here they went again. She wanted to dish on everyone else. "Where's this going, Monica?"

"He sees a lot of information in his job," she said. She shook her head slowly. "Brad's no better than a gossip columnist. He's an expert at trading one little snippet for something bigger. According to Jim, he makes more from insider stock tips than he does from his day job."

Rick blew out a slow breath as the fire of uncertainty grew within. There was only one way to put a stop to this. "I want you to come with me to talk to him. All I have is hearsay. You, on the other hand, can take away his ability to BS me."

"I can't do it. Brad can be volatile."

Now he was volatile, too? "How so? Could he have murdered Jim?"

Monica shuddered. "I don't know. I suppose it's possible. The thing is, Brad's an attention getter. He grew up on the wrong side of the tracks."

"And that means?"

"He doesn't care how others feel. He's a me-first kind of guy. But I also doubt if he's cruel or vicious. I mean, Brad's the guy who will drive across town to take a stray dog to the pound so it can be adopted by a good family. He just makes instant decisions like that. The dog needs help, get him some."

"Seriously, Monica? It sounds like you're reaching. He's dangerous, he's volatile, he's also wonderful. You're describing the perfect bad boy. How come you didn't fall in love with him?"

Rick regretted the words the second they were out of his mouth. But, enough was enough. He let his gaze bore into hers. He didn't want to argue, but he wasn't letting her continue this line of—whatever it was. Her jaw tightened until it looked like china ready to shatter.

"You really are afraid of him, aren't you?"

She wrapped her arms around herself and stared at him with watery eyes. "I told you, he can be volatile."

"He won't do anything. I promise."

"There's always later." Her voice shook as she spoke. "After we leave. Brad knows everything. He could find out—things. Ruin me."

"Let's take it one step at a time. You loved Jim, right?"

She nodded as another tear flowed down her cheek.

"Well, don't you want to know if Brad had something to do with Jim's death?"

With a puckered jaw, she seemed to consider how to answer. Rick waited, hoping she'd agree to help. Her breaths came ragged. Short bursts interrupted by chopped-up little bits. "I...I don't want to get anybody in trouble."

"You may have done that already. Look, once I tell Deputy Cunningham about this, you're involved."

The threat seemed to take her by surprise. Her resolve shattered. "The thing is, I've never seen Cadman taking drugs. I only know what Brad's told me. He's the one who told me Cadman's memory loss was caused by his oxy addiction."

35

RICK

It didn't take a genius to realize that Rick's entire conversation with Monica was a waste of time if she didn't go with him to see Brad. If she wouldn't agree to confront the man she was accusing, what was the point?

"Come with me, Monica."

She crossed her arms over her chest and glared back at Rick. "Where are you taking me?"

"To talk to Brad. I've had enough of this 'he said, she said' crap and intend to put a stop to it right now."

"I won't do it. He might want to take revenge on me."

Rick reached out, gripped her shoulders and stared her down. "Would you rather talk to the police? I can arrange that if you want."

Her expression turned blank, and she seemed to stare at nothing and everything all at once. Overhead, a pair of seagulls floated on the wind. In the distance, a sailboat cut through ocean whitecaps. And right before him, Monica stood. He hoped his gaze conveyed his need for her help. After she had a chance to think things through, she'd surely hold her silence. Right now, she saw nothing but her grief. Not the birds, the ocean. Not even him. If she didn't agree now, he risked losing her assistance.

"You want to see Jim's killer is caught, don't you?"

Rick pressed her with his stare until she glanced away. A moment later, she nodded.

"Yes," she croaked.

"So help me break down some of these walls."

Monica sucked in a breath and her color drained. "What are you going to do?"

Obviously, Bradford Luhan must have violated a host of laws against insider trading. What Rick didn't understand, or even care about, was how he got away with it. What he did want to know was what Brad's trading information had to do with Gordon's death. For that, he needed the same information Gordon had.

"I intend to invest money with Brad."

"What?" She shook her head. "You don't want to do that. It's too risky."

"I have no intention of giving him a dime, but he won't know that. I need you to make the introduction. You'll also be my insurance he tells me the same thing he told Jim. My intention is to not let him weave another wild story."

"But I don't know what he told Jim."

"Brad doesn't know that. Will you do it?"

Monica tugged on a strand of hair and stared at it. "Okay, I'll go."

"He's staying in the Jib Room. Follow me." Rick led the way, making sure Monica stayed only a few steps behind. At the door to Brad's room, he waited for her to catch up, then knocked.

The door opened a few seconds later. Brad rubbed his eyes. He greeted Rick, then Monica. Rick chose to go with the direct route, so without preamble, he launched into his first question.

"Monica tells me you gave Jim Gordon some good stock tips. How can I invest with you?"

"Whoa!" Brad raised both hands and glared at Monica. "What tall tales are you telling now, Monica?"

"She only said you'd done right by Jim." Rick glanced at her. She appeared to shrink further away as each second ticked by. "Right?"

"That's right," she echoed.

"The B&B has a little extra money that needs investing," Rick said. "Let's face it, I want to make a buck like everyone else."

"Hold on, man. What I do is connect disparate pieces of information. It's all about the timing. I've got sources everywhere."

What a line of crap, Rick thought. But he knew he had to work the source, not berate him. "So you've got a wide network. Lots of contacts. Sounds like my kind of investment opportunity. I won't lose money, will I?"

"Well, the market can be volatile. It's always a risk. This is as secure as you can get and still make a hefty profit." He shot a worried glance at Monica.

Did he expect her to disagree with him? Call him a liar? Better to let him prove it himself with a little more rope. "Thanks, Brad. I've got some big expenses coming up and could use a nice fat return. You must have a number of clients. I have to be really sure, can you give me some references?"

Luhan fingered the collar of his leather jacket and snickered. "Are you kidding me? If Monica told you about me, she got the word from Jim. There were a couple of times things got turned upside down, but Jim was ahead on balance. One satisfied customer, that's what he was. Right, Monica?"

"For the most part. Up until you two had that falling out."

"Well, like I said, the market has its ups and downs. How much are we talking about, Rick?"

"Ten grand for starters."

Brad whistled quietly and a smile spread across his face. "Nice." His eyes flicked toward Monica, then back. "When will you have the money?"

"I'll need a few more references first."

The smile disappeared and Brad backed away. "This business operates on trust, man. I keep things small. My list is private for obvious reasons. This is the sort of thing you can't discuss in public without a dozen strangers wanting in. Don't think about this too long, man. The information I've got is time sensitive. Within the next couple of days, it will be all over the news."

"What about the other treasure hunters? Are any of them clients of yours?" Rick asked.

"I don't divulge my client list. Period. It's bad for business."

To his side, Rick heard Monica mutter something unintelligible.

Brad fixed her with an intense stare, but then appeared to dismiss her. "Most of these people don't have squat." He turned his gaze on Rick. "Like Monica. She couldn't invest because she didn't have enough cash."

"Is that what Jim was doing? Investing so he could raise what he needed to find the *San Manuel*?"

"To some degree. He had different objectives at times."

"Like?"

"What do you mean, man?"

"Like what objectives?"

"Wait, are you really interested in investing or are you just sniffing for information?"

"I'm as serious as they come." Rick left off the part about finding Gordon's killer.

Brad leaned against the doorjamb, crossed his arms, and lowered his voice. "Jim made a bundle from my information. And, yes, he was using the returns from his investments to finance the hunt for the *San Manuel*. One of his objectives was to cut Reese out."

"You're quite the resource, aren't you, Brad?"

He shrugged. "I hear things."

"What can you tell me about Mr. Santiago?"

"Why?"

"You said you operate on trust. I need to know I can trust you, too."

"Heath?" Brad grimaced, then poked his head out into the hall and checked both directions before he spoke. "Hostile dude, if you ask me. He's the kind who wants everybody to look up to him. He couldn't survive if we all ignored him."

"So you didn't like him? Did Jim?"

"Jim was good at keeping Heath under control. Something happened at the end though. It had to do with this weekend, but I've got no idea what it was."

"News to me," Monica said.

"One thing's for sure, man. Heath is in this. He's got some sort of angle because Jim wasn't happy with him. And you can take that to the bank."

36

ALEX

Hey Journal,

Me and Marquetta had a good talk. She gets me better than anyone, even my dad. The way we get along is awesome. She made me see that it was wrong to spy on the guests.

I don't know how to say this, but it happened again and this time I wasn't trying to spy. Honest! I just opened my door a little and people were talking out in the hallway.

First, it was Daddy and Miss Kelley talking to Mr. Luhan. That got me to thinking about Mr. Santiago. Him and Robbie have something in common. Robbie's family has had a hard time and Mr. Santiago kept losing out to Mr. Gordon. Isn't that the same thing?

Wow, Journal, now Mr. Luhan is out in the hall with Mr. Joshua. He's telling him what happened with Daddy. I can hear what they're saying. I'm not trying to be a snoop. I promise, I'm not!

They only stayed out there for a minute. Then Mr. Joshua must've seen me cause he pulled Mr. Luhan into his room and closed the door. Since Mr. Joshua's room is next to mine, I tried that eavesdropping trick they use on the cartoons—the one with the glass. Guess what? It worked! I couldn't make out all the words, but they were definitely talking about Daddy and Mr. Gordon.

What am I gonna do now?

Alex

37

RICK

After their conversation with Brad, Rick and Monica spent a few minutes talking, then Rick returned to his office. Unable to concentrate, he decided to check on the other guests. Perhaps he could find some of them in the house.

On his way down the stairs, he spotted Marquetta coming up. She carried an armload of linens. It was part of the ritual. Everything was taken downstairs to be laundered, then had to come back up. "How come you don't use the dumbwaiter?"

"According to Devon, the less we use it, the longer it will last. This isn't a very big load, so I decided to schlep them around the hard way."

"Let me help."

She pulled to one side. "It's fine. I've got it. I was also coming to find you. Adam's in the kitchen. He's finished his route and wants to talk about the case. It doesn't sound good."

"What about you? Are you okay? You look...are you doing all right?"

His heart nearly stopped as he watched her. She caught him watching and smiled. Her gray eyes glistened. Were they moist from crying? Marquetta—always so steady—now seemed so vulnerable.

"Relax, Rick. I'll get through this. I just need some time. Now go talk to Adam."

She darted to her left and slipped by him.

"I guess Adam got Robbie home?" He called after her.

She stopped, turned sideways on the stairs and gazed down at him. This time, he was sure he did see a tear in her eye. "He didn't say anything about Robbie. You should talk to him yourself."

"Right," he muttered as she hurried on her way.

Rick found Deputy Cunningham sitting on one of the barstools at the center island sipping from a Seaside Cove B&B mug.

"What's going on, Adam?"

"Just having a little green tea for my afternoon pick-me-up."

"You actually like that stuff?"

The deputy shrugged as he gazed at his mug. "It's full of antioxidants and—other good stuff."

"Marquetta got you to say that, didn't she?"

"Don't be messing with my zen moment of the day. Hey, remember those prints we hoped to get off the monopod? There's nothing definitive other than those of Mr. Richardson. It figures that the salt water did a number on anything else that might have been there. All we've got are a few marginal partials—not enough to identify anyone. We're right back where we started."

"Too bad. There is one development you should be aware of. It concerns the return address on the envelopes. It was Gordon's, but the postmark corresponds to Cadman's address. It looks like he might have sent out the invitations to lure people here."

The deputy scratched at his temple and nodded absently. After a few moments, he smiled and said, "Terrific. We've got us some progress after all."

"Don't get too excited. Remember, Mr. Richardson has a physical limitation. Plus, it's possible Heath Santiago is somehow tied into this."

"Yuck, complications." The smile fell away and Adam sighed. "How's he related?"

"I'm not sure. It sounds like he was jealous of Gordon, but Luhan says Gordon was 'controlling' Santiago. Whatever that means."

The deputy pulled on his earlobe and grimaced. "Messy business. Okay, we keep digging."

"How long before we'll have anything from the autopsy?" Rick asked.

"At least another week. Things don't move fast around here at all."

"Never do. Anywhere. Look, what I have on Santiago might only be standard group infighting. There seems to be no love lost between any of them. The bottom line is, all Luhan said was that Santiago was involved. That doesn't mean he's the killer."

"In the interview I did, Santiago was not forthcoming at all. I wouldn't mind rattling his cage, but I've got to have grounds. You know how it works."

Rick nodded. "All too well. I've also done some thinking about the crime scene itself. Remember our initial assumption that the guests had turned the body over?"

The deputy leaned his head back so he could gaze at the ceiling. "Oh, great. Let me guess, they didn't."

"Step out back with me, Adam."

Both men went to the patio and Rick pointed at the spot where they'd found Gordon's body.

"See how rough it is down there? The surfaces are at all different kinds of steep angles. Plus, the crevices make navigating difficult. You've got to be pretty sure-footed to avoid twisting an ankle or getting trapped in those rocks."

"I see what you mean." The deputy made a move with his head somewhere between a nod and a shake, almost like he was doing figure eights. "I remember what the paramedics had to go through. You're just full of good news, aren't you? The body wasn't moved, he was hit from behind, and our prime suspect can't raise his hand above his shoulder. Oh, the dead guy didn't send the invitations, and this Santiago character is being kind of an obstructionist. Any more good news?"

"Yeah, they're all obstructionists. Or liars. It could be they don't want Gordon's murderer found for some reason."

"Cheery thought." The deputy paused for a moment, buried his face in his hands, and asked, "Anything else?"

"That's it. Oh, wait. I do have one more thing. Two, actually. It appears Monica was trying to get back together with Gordon, and Brad Luhan is using insider information to trade on the stock market." Rick snickered. "Now I'm done."

"You've turned into a royal pain in the you-know-what, Rick." Adam smiled and put a friendly hand on his shoulder. "Thanks for all your help. You've gotten much further than I ever would have."

"I had a lot of practice."

They both gazed up at the fir trees rustling in the onshore breeze. Rick suspected Adam was feeling at least as overwhelmed as he was.

"So what's our next step?" Deputy Cunningham asked.

"Wish I knew." Rick tried not to laugh, but he couldn't stop himself. "I am so stumped. Given the way these people are lying and turning on each other, we should probably resort to some good old-fashioned blackmail. I've tried getting information on them, but didn't find much. Maybe if you run background checks you'll turn up something. That might tell us who's got something to hide and who doesn't. With that, we might be able to plow our way through this."

"Give me a couple of hours. I'll see what I can turn up. In the meantime, keep digging. You might crack this case yet."

38

RICK

Marquetta was standing at the kitchen center island watching Rick and Deputy Cunningham as they entered. She had the suggestion of a smile on her face, and Rick was sure she had something on her mind.

"What are you so amused about?" Rick asked.

"You two look like two little boys who crashed their new drone."

"Drone?" Rick grinned at Adam. "I had a remote-controlled airplane once, but a drone—well, that would have been awesome."

"I didn't even get the airplane. My dad was always making me practice my piano lessons. I hated it."

"Piano?" Rick shook his head. "Ouch. Your old man was a real taskmaster."

The deputy's right cheek inched up and he nodded. "It's no wonder I'm so screwed up."

Marquetta glared at Adam. "Your dad was a nice man."

"You didn't live with him, Marky." The deputy rolled his eyes. "Oy. Anyway, I'll keep you posted when I find out something," he said as he left.

Rick grabbed a glass of water, eager to share what he'd learned with Marquetta. "I asked Adam to run background checks on the guests."

"Getting into the role, are you?" Marquetta winked and smiled. "Actually, it's a good idea. We really don't know anything about these people when they come here. But when something like this happens, it makes you wonder."

"More than wonder. My stomach is in knots over what one of them could do to Alex." He lowered his voice. "I never worried about raising my daughter in a place where there would always be strangers. It never occurred to me that there could be danger until you called to tell me about Gordon. I guess we don't know who's staying here until something bad happens."

"In some ways, that's true. But, you get to meet new people every single day. I find it kind of exciting."

"It has been that."

She picked up a towel and dried the granite around the sink. "Where's Alex?"

"Actually, I haven't seen her in a while. I need to check on her in a bit. Our end-of-day ritual starts in about half an hour. Dinner for two." He tried not to wince. The comment had come out filled with self-pity—not what he'd intended at all.

"You two have some things to talk about tonight, I'm sure."

His cheeks warmed with embarrassment over what might happen in the next few seconds. Would she say yes? Or no? "I'd like you to stay. For dinner. If you want to. I mean, you're so good with Alex and…"

"I'd be happy to."

He licked his lips, unable to believe she'd agreed. He was acting like a tongue-tied schoolboy, his mind, nothing but a blank.

"Are you okay, Rick?"

"Yes! I'm great." He surveyed the countertops in hopes of finding a topic of conversation. But, everything had been put away and the only things left in sight were two loaves of Chocolate Chip Banana Bread. "Are those for tomorrow morning?"

She snickered. "What's up with you? You know the routine. Each afternoon I prepare something for the following day. That way, we're ready. Surely you have it figured out by now."

"You're right. I knew that." Without thinking, he said, "If you've got a minute, can we go outside and talk?"

She frowned, then nodded. "Sure. Just let me finish. I have to leave in a few minutes." She quickly added, "But I'll come back after I run a couple of errands."

"Sounds good."

He stood to the side while she placed both loaves into the ceramic bread box. When she'd replaced the lid, she wiped up a few rogue crumbs, then inclined her head toward the door.

"Ladies first," he said.

She curtsied and led the way to the patio. The afternoon air held a misty quality. Gray cloaked everything to the west and dampened the colors. The shoreline had gone from sunny to foggy so slowly he hadn't even noticed. At least the inland side remained clear.

"I can't get used to this," Rick said.

The comment earned him a raised eyebrow and a craned neck.

"This is what you call June Gloom, right? You people who have lived along the California coast all your lives are used to it. I'm still trying to sort out what layer to wear when."

Marquetta giggled. "Don't worry. You're not alone. No matter how long you live here, you'll never be prepared for Mother Nature's surprises. Even the weatherman can't get it right."

Their footsteps were slow, deliberate. They walked side-by-side, seemingly in perfect harmony. Her pace matched his. She hugged her arms to her chest, causing him to glance over his shoulder at the B&B.

"Let me go back and get a coat for you," he said.

"I'm okay. Where are we going?"

"Down by the water?"

She nodded, and they started down the paved walkway to the shore. The gentle slope was an easy walk and neither seemed in a hurry. Rick's pulse raced. He felt such a strong connection with her. In that moment, he realized nothing else mattered. He didn't need facts. History. Background. He understood the most important thing of all—she was the kind of woman he could fall in love with.

When he stopped walking, so did she. He turned to her and saw worry lines on her forehead not normally there. She averted her gaze, and he gave her space by looking away.

He took a small step backwards and focused on the moon hanging over the horizon in the eastern sky. "Moon's coming up." He smiled at her. "It looks like an egg standing on end."

Marquetta's eyes glistened, and she looked at the sky. "It's a waxing gibbous moon. Some call it the 'moon of endings.'"

"Does that mean you won't be staying?" His breath caught. He hadn't meant to ask that question, but it had popped out. Now, he had to wait for her answer. It seemed to take forever.

"I don't know what it means. I've been here a long time. I thought after our talk it would be better, but I'm not sure." She sniffled, shook her head. "There are circumstances I may never be able to reconcile."

"Maybe I can help."

"I don't think so."

"Does your uncertainty have to do with me asking Joe Gray about your father?"

She paused, gazed at the moon again, and rested her hand on her throat.

His heart thumped in his chest so fast he could barely breathe. "I'm sorry I intruded. It was wrong of me."

"There are other things, Rick. Things I can't talk about."

Can't? Or won't? "I don't care. Nothing from the past matters."

"Now you sound like Alex." She gave him a weak smile and avoided his gaze again.

"We can work through it—whatever it is."

She gripped her sides harder, but gave him no answer. Was she lowering her defenses, or simply cold? He reached out and touched her chin with his fingers. Lifted it until her eyes met his.

"Nothing else matters," he whispered.

Marquetta turned her head aside and the creases in her forehead deepened. She sniffled again and took in a sharp breath. "I told you. I can't. It's not my story to tell. I'm sorry."

He extended his hand again, but she pulled away.

"Let's call it a day, okay? There's so much going on tomorrow. You have a murder to solve, and I have all these people to keep happy." She wiped away an imaginary tear. "See you in the morning."

She left so abruptly he was unable to think or say anything other than a reluctant, "Right. Tomorrow."

He waited while she rushed up the path toward the house. When she disappeared inside, his gaze darted up to the moon, and his emotions struggled to find solid ground.

"I can't take another ending," he said into the breeze. For a moment, he glared at the rocks where Jim Gordon had died, then the waxing gibbous moon and the house left to him by his grandfather. Finally, he simply stood watching the ocean, counting seconds between waves, and kept asking the same question. "What kinds of secrets did you have, Captain Jack?"

39

ALEX

June 17

Hey Journal,

I'm up in my room cause I'm sad and don't want to talk to anybody. I moved my chair so I can look out the window. That kinda helps, but it sucks cause my dad is making a huge mistake. He likes that Miss Potok. He's so wrong about her.

Daddy and Marquetta belong together. I didn't see that before, but now I do.

I stop writing cause I'm not sure what to say next. When I look out the window, Daddy and Marquetta are out on the patio. Talking. It looks like they might be going for a walk.

My eyes are watery and I guess it's cause I'm so happy. I pick up my journal and draw a big heart on the page. In the middle of the heart, I write "Daddy & Marquetta." The page gets all blurry again, but I start to write anyway.

Holy moly, Journal. It's happening. My wish is coming true.

I'm like so happy. It's gonna be totally awesome when Marquetta marries Daddy and becomes my mom. It's the same way

I always dreamed it would be with my mom and dad. I feel stupid now for trying to set him up with Bella. She's nice, but she never paid a lot of attention to me or my dad. But, Marquetta's always cool. She's the one who told me I should write down my innermost thoughts. And right now I got a bunch of them.

This could be that reverse psychology thing Daddy talks about sometimes. He says you can make somebody do something by telling them to do the opposite. Maybe that's what happened with him and Miss Potok. Daddy doesn't like being manipulated. He said that's what my mom always did, and he never wants it to happen again. I never asked what he meant by it. Maybe I get how he feels now.

I gotta find a way to prove Miss Potok is doing the same thing my mom used to do. If I don't, I could wind up like those kids in the movies. You know, the ones who get sent away cause their new stepmom wants them to go to boarding school.

This time when I look outside Marquetta's running this way. But my dad's still down by the water. She stops at the edge of the patio and looks back. When she turns around, she's got tears running down her cheeks. What happened? Did they have a fight? No way! I gotta stop her before she leaves.

I push my chair back and run out the door.

At the top of the stairs, I see her. She's on her way to the front door.

"Marquetta! Wait!"

She doesn't hear me. If I hurry down there, I can stop her.

My ankle slips.

Somebody screams. Me?

My back hits something hard. "Ow!"

There's the ceiling. And the floor.

The ceiling again.

When I open my eyes, Marquetta is holding me. My fingers touch her arm. "You're real..."

"Alex? Are you okay?"

"I think so. My ankle. It hurts. Bad. My back, too."

"Why were you running down the stairs?"

"I had to stop you before you left."

She hugs me. I lean my head into her arm. It's soft. Warm. And the pain is a little better.

"How many fingers?"

"Five."

"I was holding up two."

"Yeah, but you have five. Ow, that hurts. Ow, ow...I can't laugh."

A man walks up and stands over us. I smile at him. "Hi, Deputy Cunningham."

"What the heck happened here?" He kneels down and touches my ankle. "I don't think it's broken. To be safe, we should get an x-ray."

"Let's hope she only twisted it," Marquetta says.

"I'm gonna be okay now."

"Adam, can you carry her into the kitchen?"

"Sure. Come on, munchkin."

He groans as he lifts me. "Oh, wow, you're getting heavy." Then, he carries me into the kitchen and puts me on the island.

"Awesome! I've never sat on the counter before."

"Don't try it again, either."

Marquetta tries to sound mean, but I can tell she's totally worried about me.

"It's just a few bumps and bruises," Deputy Cunningham says.

"We need to tell Rick what's happened. Adam, would you get him? He's down by the shore."

"Sure thing. Be right back."

Once Deputy Cunningham is out of the room, Marquetta looks at me. Her eyes are all red.

"Now, tell me why you were running down those stairs."

I gotta admit, Marquetta is super intimidating. She's totally intense. So I tell her about Daddy and Miss Potok and then I tell her how I heard Mr. Joshua and Mr. Luhan talking and what they were saying. And most of all, how I'm afraid she's gonna leave us.

When I'm done, she clears her throat and goes to the window. "Where's your dad? Why isn't Adam back already?"

"You're gonna tell Daddy everything, aren't you?"

She comes and sits on one of the stools. "Yes, Sweetie. I have to. Actually, you're the one who should do that."

I hang my head. "I know. Is he gonna send me away?"

Marquetta doesn't seem to understand. "Where would he send you? Better yet, why would you think he'd do that?"

"Because I've been doing what he said I shouldn't." My eyes burn and my voice is all creaky. "He's probably tired of me. My mom got tired of me. He probably is, too."

She holds me until I stop shaking. "Sweetheart, your dad loves you more than you could possibly know. He will never leave you. He might discipline you when you're in the wrong, but he won't ever give up on you." A couple of her tears drip from her cheek onto my shirt. She wipes at her cheek and sucks in a quick breath. "And neither will I."

Oh my God. Does she mean what I think she does? "You're not going away?"

"No, Sweetie. I won't leave you."

I can't stop myself from burying my face in her shoulder and blubbering like a baby. "I wish Daddy was here."

"I don't understand why they're not back yet. Sweetie, you stay right there while I go check on them."

"Okay."

She slips away and I wrap my arms around my knees. My ankle's swollen, but I'm totally okay now. Marquetta's staying. I rock back and forth on the counter. I haven't been so warm and happy inside for such a long time. We're gonna be like a real family.

And then Marquetta screams. She runs to the patio door.

"Stay where you are, Alex. Don't move!"

40

RICK

Rick stood on the spot where they discovered Jim Gordon's body. The same question still nagged at him. He'd gone back and forth in his reasoning, but the bottom line was he had to know how Gordon got on this rock. It was several feet above the ocean and perfectly dry, yet his clothes had been wet.

With the tide out, the ocean's surface lay two feet below the top of the rock closest to the water. But, larger incoming surges washed right over the tops. Rick hopped carefully from one boulder to the next to get closer. He stood looking straight down at the water. An incoming wave slammed into his ankles. He tottered on the slippery surface, but kept his balance.

As the water swirled through the crevices and gradually drained back to the sea, he also wondered if it was even possible for a man to climb out without help.

He had to know. Everything depended on that one answer. If it was possible for Gordon to have made it out on his own, the killer might be anyone. If he needed help, it would have taken a strong man. That would narrow the list of suspects. He took a deep breath. Steeled himself for the next surge.

It came.

Retreated.

He watched. Contemplated. So much force. He had to return to safety.

A movement caught his attention, and he turned toward shore to see who was coming. It was Adam.

The roar of another surge filled the air.

Rick whirled around. White foam curled forward into a powerful waterfall. This one approached with frightening speed. Adam yelled, but the approaching roar drowned out his words. Rick stared at the wave approaching. It could easily knock him off his feet. He braced himself, but the wave hit a with a power stronger than anything he could have imagined.

In the momentary silence when the wave reversed direction, he heard Adam yell. "Get out of there!"

But instead of taking a step back, Rick struggled just to maintain his balance. His legs quivered. The force sucking him away from shore intensified. His pulse raced. The strength of the pull grew. One foot slipped, and he jumped to avoid falling onto the rocks.

The tide pulled him ten feet in seconds. The shock of landing in a sixty-degree ocean drove the breath from his lungs. He spit out salt water and forced himself to inhale. His eyes burned, and he choked as he took in more water. Desperate to find a point of reference, he kicked furiously.

The B&B appeared in his vision. Home. Safety.

Cold seeped through his clothing and skin to his bones. It was impossible to breathe normally. His breaths came machine-gun fast. His thoughts fragmented. The current shoved him wherever it wanted. Fighting it wasted energy. He had to keep a point of reference. The house. Stay with it. It's the beacon. The force that would keep him alive.

It held his life. Marquetta. Alex.

Oh God, no. Was Alex watching? Would she see him die?

Rick's teeth chattered as the next frigid wave carried him toward the rocks.

Adam stood where Rick had been pulled in. Rick's pulse raged almost as loud as the tide. He twisted sideways just as he slammed into a massive boulder. Excruciating pain shot through his spine as he caromed off the rocks.

Above, a hand reached for him. But it was too far away. Rick thrashed toward Adam, but the tide dragged him further away. Already the bone-chilling cold dulled his senses. The pull lessened. This was the lull he'd expected before. The moment the flow reversed direction.

He swam to his left. A wave caught his body and propelled him forward. He got his feet in front of him. Kicked against the driving force. Another waste of energy. His foot hit the rocks and slid off even as his hand scraped against a rough surface. He tried to grab hold, but it was slimy and impossible to grip.

Adam still lay on the rock reaching out. But his hand was so far up. Rick promised that if he got out of this, he was changing his life. He had to do it. For Alex. For himself.

Rick kicked and reached up with one hand. Adam seized Rick's wrist. It felt like his arm had been yanked it out of its socket.

"Pull, Rick! Or we're both dead men."

The tide sucked against his body like a giant vacuum. Rick heaved against the seaward siphon until only his feet were in the water. Sheets cascaded from his clothing as he hung above the trough, but they were still within reach of the next crest.

The deputy's grip anchored him as he found a crevice with his right foot. He pushed down and stumbled forward, then collapsed on a rock. His body shook uncontrollably, and he gasped for air. Adam landed on the rock next to him. Rick looked around. He was safe on a boulder high and dry. Just like Jim Gordon had been.

Everything ached. He coughed out seawater and inhaled short gulps of air. The rock's warmth did nothing to lessen the cold deep in his bones. He lay there, his pulse still pounding in his ears.

Adam leaned on his elbows, gasping. "What in God's name were you trying to prove?"

"I got too close." Another chill coursed through Rick's spine. "Thank you. You saved my life."

"You almost got us both killed."

Another wave washed over the rock Rick had stood on when he'd been thrown off-balance. It might have only been moments before, but right now it felt like a lifetime away. Another shiver ran through him. "That water is freaking frigid." A few seconds later, he added, "Sorry, Adam. I had a theory. At least now I know."

"What? What was so important you had to pull a stunt like that?"

"It's all crystal clear now. When Gordon was out there, he was probably scared to death. He would have done or said anything to save himself."

"You had to risk your life to figure that out?" Adam laughed over the crash of another wave. "And here I thought you were a smart guy. Didn't anyone around here ever tell you to never turn your back on the ocean?"

Rick chuckled. "Guess not. Thanks for sharing."

Adam groaned. His body shook as he got up on one knee. "Everything hurts. We're both lucky to be alive."

"I can barely move. Gordon must have been the same way. You know what that means, right?"

"That you're the luckiest guy alive," Deputy Cunningham said.

"I'd agree with that, but it also means Gordon didn't pull himself out. He had to have help. And it had to be a man—someone big enough and strong enough to not be pulled in, too."

"So you're theory is this Good Samaritan helped him out and then killed him? That's weird."

"Adam, I'd bet almost anything Gordon made a promise to save his life. I sure did. We just have to figure out what that promise was."

"Fat lot of good it did him."

Adam extended a shaky hand to help Rick up. Rick's knees trembled too much to stand on his own, so they steadied each other as they made their way across the rocks.

"I suspect Gordon changed his mind the minute he was on dry land. Whoever he made the promise to was probably furious after they saved him, and he reneged. There's only one thing I can think of that would have caused that kind of reaction, Adam."

"Losing the treasure they're all after?"

"I'm not sure the murder had anything to do with the treasure. This was deeply personal."

41

RICK

Rick turned at the sound of running footsteps. Marquetta raced toward them, a mask of fear covering her face. With Adam's help, Rick inched in her direction. He wanted to embrace her and assure her he hadn't been trying to kill himself. He reached out, but she stopped short.

"Are you out of your mind?" Marquetta glared at him.

"I'm sorry. I didn't realize how stupid it was to get so close."

She clasped her arms around her. "When I saw you, I thought I was going to...Alex was going to lose you."

A little tinge of warmth filled Rick's insides. She cared. "I'm here."

Marquetta snapped, "Alex needs you." She glanced up at the B&B. Rick followed her gaze. Alex stood on one leg, using the back of an Adirondack chair as a brace while she kept her other foot off the ground.

"What happened?" Rick asked.

"That's what I was trying to tell you when you decided to go bodysurfing," Adam said. "She took a little tumble down the stairs."

"Is she hurt?"

"If you hadn't survived...ooh, men!" Marquetta stalked back toward the house.

Supported by Deputy Cunningham, Rick hobbled up the path. His knees trembled as they walked. Adam advised him to slow down, but Rick kept pushing and didn't stop until he stumbled onto the patio and held Alex in his arms.

A shudder ran through her body. The magnitude of his mistake slammed into Rick just as the tide had driven him into the rocks. "I'm so sorry, Alex. I don't know what I was thinking."

"I was afraid you were gonna die, Daddy."

"No, kiddo. I had no intention of dying." And yet, he'd done something so stupid it could have happened easily. "Everything's okay now. We're all fine."

He wrapped himself in a beach towel Marquetta handed him and collapsed into the nearest chair. Alex crawled onto his lap as Marquetta and Adam watched them. The others appeared completely drained, much like he felt. Marquetta held her hand over her mouth. It appeared she might burst into tears at any moment.

"I'm sorry I gave you all a scare," Rick said. "I had this theory about Gordon's murder. Everything seemed to hinge on whether he made it out of that water on his own."

Alex leaned back and peered at him. "Why's that matter, Daddy?"

"If Mr. Gordon pulled himself out, it would mean he laid there on the rocks until someone came along and killed him. But, if he had help getting out it would have been..."

"A crime of passion!" Alex squealed.

"Oh, Lordy, what a world we live in."

Rick blew out a slow breath and nodded at Marquetta. "I agree." He glanced at Deputy Cunningham, who looked grim.

"So our original theory that the others turned the body over isn't possible," the deputy said. "And you think our killer is a strong man who murdered Gordon because he was angered. Plus, we're throwing out the lost treasure angle."

"You may not want to discard that theory quite yet," Marquetta said. "We might have something."

Rick glanced at her, then Alex. "We?"

"Precisely," Marquetta said as she nodded at Alex.

"Daddy? There's something I have to tell you."

Alex rocked back and forth on Rick's lap, each tiny movement a painful reminder of how much his body would ache for the next few days.

"Okay, kiddo. What's up?"

"Mr. Luhan and Mr. Joshua are friends."

"Of course they are. They're here as part of the same group."

"Hello," Alex became more insistent. "They're friends. Like BFFs. They talk and hang out together. And they were talking about what Mr. Luhan said to you."

"Really? Are you sure about this?" Rick shrugged and cleared his throat. He was too tired to be angry with Alex for spying again. They could deal with that issue later after things returned to something resembling normal. He gently shook her shoulder. "It's okay. You can tell me."

"I was in my own room so it's not like I broke in or anything. Honest."

"It's okay, Alex. Tell me. Whatever it is."

"They were in the hallway. When they saw me, they snuck into Mr. Joshua's room."

"That's not spying, kiddo."

Alex scrunched up her face. "Yeah, but I might've kinda sorta listened in using a glass on the wall."

Rick rotated his neck in little circles to ease the tension. For one tiny instant, he felt the motion of his body in the water. How helpless he'd been. He wrapped his arms around Alex and embraced her. "We'll talk about eavesdropping when I'm not quite so exhausted. For now, is there anything else I should be aware of?"

"They argued some more." She quickly added, "But I didn't hear anything special."

"Too bad," Deputy Cunningham grumbled. "It would have helped to know what happened in that conversation."

"I agree," Rick said. Alex's observation seemed a bit of a stretch, but so was everything else with this group.

"So you'd be happy if I found something else?" Alex's tone escalated from subdued to excited.

"Found? I can tell right now I'm not going to like this, am I?" He looked to Marquetta for an indication of what was to come, but her expression was also blank.

"She only told me about the conversation in the hallway. Sweetie, what else do you know?"

Alex pursed her lips. "I need immunity."

"You what?" Rick blinked and stared at her. "What did you do, Alex?"

"You gotta promise."

"This is not a negotiation, young lady." To the side, he heard Adam snicker. "Don't you encourage her," Rick snapped.

"We need a break, Rick. What have you got, munchkin?"

"I won't get in trouble?"

"Not from me," Deputy Cunningham said.

Rick huffed. "Fine. Promise. You've got your immunity. This time."

"Miss Potok's lying to you, Daddy."

"I understand you don't like her, Alex. But that's no reason to call her a liar."

Alex shook her head. "That's not it. I'm positive she's lying cause of what me and Robbie found in her room."

"Oh, God," Marquetta muttered.

Rick closed his eyes and muttered, "What now?" Mentally, he counted to five. "And what would that be, Alex?"

"A totally different treasure map. She's got a whole map hidden under her bed."

42

ALEX

The adults are all staring at me like I just made myself disappear or something. "It's true! Me and Robbie found a treasure map under Miss Potok's bed."

"This is a lot to take in, kiddo. How big was the map?"

"It's like the size of the town tourist map." I hold out my hands to show them.

"And it was complete? There were no missing parts?"

I nod.

Daddy looks at Deputy Cunningham. "And you thought I was the one with all the good news."

"We'll need to see this map," Deputy Cunningham says.

My dad scratches his left eyebrow like he does when he's figuring something out. "Maybe she's behind the weekend," he says. "I wonder if it's the same map everybody's got a part of, or it's something different altogether." He looks at me. "You didn't have any way of comparing this new map to any others, did you Alex?"

I shake my head.

"Let's put that on the back burner for a moment," Daddy says. "Alex is correct, Luhan and Joshua are friends. That's a connection. But you didn't hear them say anything about killing Gordon, did you Alex?"

He looks right at me and I stick out my lower lip. "No. I guess I messed up." Rats. I wish I had listened more. And I totally wish me and Robbie had taken a picture of the map.

"It's okay, kiddo. We're still trying to piece together the parts in this puzzle. Look, we also know Monica wanted to be with Gordon. And, the animosity between Gordon and Richardson might have been thick, but we can eliminate both of them. Richardson's injury takes him out of the running, and Monica's too weak."

"That's pretty sexist." Marquetta doesn't look happy with my dad.

Deputy Cunningham shakes his head at Marquetta. "It's nothing sexist at all."

"Adam saw how hard it was to get me out of that water." Daddy leans back in the chair. He looks like he's in a lot of pain. I bet getting beat up by the ocean really hurts.

"It couldn't have been a woman who saved him," Deputy Cunningham says. "No way. Gordon wasn't a huge man, but he weighed enough to pull a rescuer in with him—unless that person weighed more than him or was really strong. And both of these female treasure hunters are pretty slight. I think either of them would have been yanked in if they tried to rescue him. Just based on the physics, it had to be Luhan or Kalstone."

"It doesn't eliminate them as a killer," Marquetta says.

This is totally cool. We're like brainstorming about the murder. "What about Mr. Santiago?"

"What about him, kiddo?"

"He didn't like Mr. Gordon either."

Daddy moves me a little to one side. "Ugh, leg cramp. Anyway, that's right. Santiago didn't like Gordon at all."

"Did any of these people get along?" Deputy Cunningham looks at Daddy, then Marquetta, and then me. "This reminds me of elementary school."

"This is worse than school." I roll my eyes.

Marquetta holds up her hand, palm out, and we high-five each other.

"Good analogy, Sweetie."

"What's an analogy?"

"It's when one thing is compared to another," Marquetta says.

"Why do you say this is worse, kiddo?"

"Cause in school Trey Quintana likes to tell everybody's secrets. But Trey doesn't hurt anybody. Most of the kids don't like Trey cause they don't trust him. I think he just wants attention and the only way he knows how to get it is to cause trouble."

My dad leans back and peers at me for a few seconds. "You know what, kiddo? You're pretty smart."

"Thanks, Daddy."

He winks at me before he looks at Deputy Cunningham. "Adam, when I was talking to Monica, she accused Brad of insider trading. And when I asked Cadman how he knew his monopod was down in the rocks, he said a little birdie told him. That birdie has to be Brad, and he's our Trey Quintana."

43

RICK

The comparison of Brad Luhan to one of Alex's classmates struck Rick as unlikely when he first heard the words. However, as he watched Alex's face and listened to her sincerity, he realized the idea had merit. In fact, the more he considered the comparison, the more he liked it. The beauty was it also gave him a way to proceed.

He gave Alex's ponytail a little tug. "Like I said, pretty smart. Adam, I'm sure Brad's not our killer, but I'll bet he knows who is. He was vague when I asked him about his information sources. I'm pretty sure he won't willingly give up what he knows. But, if we twist the screws we might get enough to help us move forward. He doesn't strike me as the type to help the law. Quite the contrary, I expect him to use that information to blackmail our killer."

"You're supposed to be helping, Rick, not telling me how bad things are. If he's a blackmailer, this is going to get even more convoluted."

"You're right. That's why I want to talk to Reese first."

Alex straightened up. The shift in weight sent shooting pains through Rick's thighs and up his spine. She hung her head and snuggled closer. "Do you have to talk to her?"

"Yes, because I'm sure she and Mr. Gordon were involved romantically. If I'm correct, this will give us leverage to use on Mr. Luhan. Let's see if it will help us break open the gossip piggybank he's guarding so well."

Marquetta agreed to watch Alex while Rick went inside to change. On his way through the lobby, he found Reese hunched over her laptop on one of the gray couches. Sunlight streamed through the window to her right, but she seemed oblivious to it. She continued typing as he approached. When he cleared his throat, she looked up, eyed him and pointed at his damp clothes.

"Nice look."

He glanced down. At least he was no longer dripping water. "I was on my way upstairs, but saw you sitting here. You looked pretty intense."

"I'm working on a recovery plan." She paused, exhaled deliberately, then continued. "For the *San Manuel* and my reputation."

"So you found the ship?"

"Not that kind of recovery."

"You no longer believe in it?"

"I do. It's out there. All I'm doing is shifting from Plan A to B."

Right. Plan B. It was probably tied to the map Alex had found. He narrowed his gaze. "Does that mean your fellow treasure hunters are out of luck?"

She regarded the scene outside the window—roses basking in dappled sunlight, palm tree leaves swaying in the breeze. "It means they're on their own."

"You're leaving them to fend for themselves."

"If you want to be blunt."

"Don't you mean honest?"

"Whatever."

"You described some of your research to Joe Gray. It sounded legitimate to me, so why does Monica give you so little credit for what you've done? She implied you were sleeping with Jim, but when we talked, you said you two were just casual."

181

She closed the lid on her laptop and sat back. "Monica's jealous because things between her and Jim were falling apart."

"Because?"

Reese rolled her eyes, then glared at him. "Because we did 'do the nasty.' If you must know, it was twice to be exact. Huge mistake. We got caught up in the moment. It was this stupid weekend fling. Nothing more."

Now he believed her. This was the real Reese Potok. A little surge of irritation reminded him how he, too, had been taken in. "You have a broad definition of casual."

"Excuse me?"

Rick moved closer. He put a hand on the back of the couch and stared down at her. "Is there anything else you left out?"

She didn't answer. Of course not. Why would she tell him about Plan B? She probably didn't trust him any more than her fellow treasure hunters. Though he didn't trust her either, there was something about her. If only he could put his finger on it.

She peered at him with blue eyes that almost seemed to beg forgiveness. "I've disappointed you, haven't I?"

"I'm not sure," he said. "Right now, I'm trying to find a killer. That's all."

The smile fell from her face and the corners of her lips turned down into a frown. "I'm sorry."

"For?"

"Disappointing you."

The last thing he wanted to do was burn bridges unnecessarily. He still might need Reese as a source—and there was that air of mystery about her. He reached out, touched her shoulder, and said, "The good news is I don't think you're the killer."

She leaned back and sighed. "That's a relief. What makes you so sure?"

"Let's say Deputy Cunningham and I have narrowed the list based on the laws of physics. The deceased's clothing was soaked as though he'd taken a dunk in the ocean." Rick spread his hands to his sides and smiled. "It would have been physically impossible for you to pull him out."

"The deceased? It sounds so...sterile. And that's how you got wet? You jumped in the ocean?"

"Sorry. You're right about the jargon. I learned it when I was a reporter. Anyway, I accidentally tested my theory and I'm almost positive you're not the killer."

She pursed her lips and nodded. "I guess that lets out Monica, too?"

"If you want another cliché, it would have taken someone who was big and strong. In other words, our list is down to the four guys. The most likely ones are Brad and Hayden."

"And you're telling me this why?"

His jaw tightened. Good question. He smiled, "You know these people better than I do. I'd like some insight into what Brad actually does."

"Does? As in work?" She snickered. "Not much from what I've seen." She paused and batted her eyes at him. "Sorry, that wasn't nice. Anyway, he likes that whole bad boy image—you've seen it, leather jacket, chain necklace."

"Tell me something not so obvious."

"He loves that nose ring of his. It really disturbs me—piercing your nose. Yuck."

"Not helpful."

"He grew up on the wrong side of the tracks and learned to survive by trading information. How's that?"

"Better, but I already knew about it."

"My, my, you are thorough."

Reese paused and gazed across the room for a few seconds before looking back at him and continuing.

"How about this? Brad and Mark have some sort of thing going. I'm not sure exactly what it is, but I've seen them. You know how people put their heads together and keep their voices low when they're keeping a secret? Well, they've been doing that for a while now. I suppose it could be related to the stock trading thing, but Brad was never so secretive with Jim. These two—it's something different."

"How much help has Brad been in finding the *San Manuel*?"

"None. In my opinion, the only reason he's here is to expand his network."

Rick frowned and thought back to his discussion with Brad. Too many complicated puzzle pieces and none of them made sense. "When I talked to him, Brad told me he thought Heath was somehow involved in Jim's death. Do you feel the same way?"

"Heath is a very hostile guy. He's different from Brad. He could be involved. I can't tell you for sure."

"Is Brad hostile?"

"Brad is greedy. He likes money and recognition—and not necessarily in that order. Strange guy. With most people it's one or the other. Not him. It's like somebody flips a switch."

"And you? What is it you want? Is it just the *San Manuel* like you told Joe Gray?"

"That's a hard question."

"Let's cut to the chase. Do you want something more than the *San Manuel*?"

"A girl can dream, right? The whole treasure thing is so sexy. The idea of seeing my name in print as the one who found it— that's pretty amazing."

He hadn't expected anything more. Reese was driven. Maybe too much so. Is that why she was hiding the other map? "Everyone here seems to blame Jim for something. What about you?"

She laughed and shook her head. "The number of people in this group who didn't have an ax to grind with Jim can be counted without using any fingers."

"Meaning zero?"

"Jim was the kind of guy who eventually took advantage of everyone."

"So you wanted the world to recognize your research uncovered the *San Manuel*, not his."

"Yes."

Finally, he had a straight answer. "So you hated him?"

"Mild contempt. Especially after...that weekend."

"Because?"

"Because that's when he stole my research. It was when I decided he was a despicable human being who should be removed from the face of the earth. I'm still trying to figure out whether I'm happy or sad he's dead."

"I'm surprised. If you disliked him so much, I'd expect you to be happy."

"I am, but I'm sad because someone beat me to it."

44

RICK

Rick stared at Reese for a long moment, recalling the times in his life when he'd hated someone enough to contemplate murder. Those instances, though few and far between, did exist. Whether he never acted on the urge due to a fear of being caught or his own moral code, he wasn't sure. Someone, however, had followed through. Did one of these people hate Gordon enough to plan his murder? Or had this been what Alex called it? A crime of passion.

"Let's get back to Brad for a minute," he said.

"Why don't you talk to him directly?" She shrugged. "Aren't I what you would call an unreliable source?"

"This is for background. I'll be getting to him. Is Brad tight with anyone else in the group?"

"Hmmm...maybe Hayden. They've been spending more time together lately. Like I said, Brad likes to build his network."

Hayden. Brad. Mark. Monica. Where to start? Probably with Brad. If he ran into a wall, he could fall back to one of the others and see where the process took him. He heard a woman's voice upstairs. It was Monica's, and she sounded irate.

"Liar!"

Rick rushed to the staircase despite his growing aches and pains. Monica stood on the top landing next to Brad. Even from one flight down the angry flush in her cheeks burned bright.

"What's going on here?" Rick asked as he climbed the stairs.

Brad's eyes flicked toward Monica, then Rick. "She's off the rails, man. I got no idea what she's talking about."

"You know exactly what this is about, Brad." Monica shot a glance at Rick. "He's trying to tell me Jim stopped investing with him. Jim told me all his money was tied up in investments and those two were thick as thieves when it came to making money."

Brad snickered. "You got it all wrong, Monica. Jim and I were done."

"Why?" Rick asked.

"Let's just say he didn't appreciate the result the last time we did a deal."

"So how much money did he lose on this supposed solid investment?" Rick asked.

"Everything."

Rick shivered. Yes, he was still wearing wet clothes. Yes, he was freezing his butt off. But what really got him was that Captain Jack had done exactly the same thing. He gambled everything on one roll of the dice and Rick was now stuck with the payback. "You're telling me your stock tip cost Jim Gordon everything he had. Is that what you're saying?"

Monica's jaw fell as she stared at Rick. "Jim was broke?"

Rick ignored her. "What did he do, Brad, threaten to report you for insider trading?"

The man's face went stone cold. He swallowed hard and avoided eye contact. When he spoke, his voice was smooth and calm. "No, nothing like that. Jim was a big boy. He realized the risks of investing."

Quick recovery, thought Rick. Time to press harder. "Especially when you're dealing with illegal information?"

Monica's eyes narrowed to a laser-like focus. "So the rumor's true? You really did cost him everything?"

"Shut up, Monica." Brad leaned closer to her. "You knew nothing about what was going on." His voice turned razor sharp. "Or what Jim was really like."

Rick clutched his towel tighter as he took the final step to the top of the landing and faced off against Brad. "Tell me. What was he like?"

"Ruthless. Dude was as mean as they get." His eyes cut sideways to Monica. "He just kept her around to pass the time."

"You liar, we were getting married."

"Nice little fantasy, Monica. It was never going to happen."

Her lower lip quivered. "No...you're just trying to upset me."

"There's no need for anyone to work hard on that one." Brad puffed up his shoulders and snickered. "You go all drama queen when your coffee's too hot."

Before Monica could respond, Rick leaned forward until his face was inches from Brad's. "She's never complained about ours."

Brad shrunk back from his aggressive stance and rolled his neck in the way people do to loosen up. "Yeah, well, it's just a figure of speech."

"How about you give me a figure of speech for your arrangement with Jim?"

"Finished," he said, matter-of-factly.

"Did you argue?"

"Some."

"Would you rather talk to the SEC?"

Brad scowled at Rick. It was the kind of signal Rick had hoped for. He finally had exactly what he wanted, Brad on the run.

"You wouldn't," he stammered.

"You've probably violated more laws than I can count. I might ask the FBI to pay you a visit, too."

"Okay, okay. Let's take a step back. We can keep this low key. Sorry if I got a little carried away."

"What happened with Jim?"

Brad took a deep breath and looked around. "This is between you and me. She needs to leave." He inclined his head toward Monica.

"She stays. I want a witness in case you decide to change your story. Start talking or I start dialing."

After a long pause during which Brad chewed on his lower lip, the words began to tumble out. "One of my tips was wrong. I'd heard this software company had a deal in the works with the US Navy for this super-secret app. The source had contacts involved in the procurement process on the inside. Don't you see, man? This was the score of a lifetime. A no-name company gets a contract worth millions and the stock goes through the roof. I told Jim about it. He needed money to finance the expedition. I tried to warn him about the pitfalls of leveraging his money, but he wanted to go big."

"Don't BS me, Brad. I've dealt with inside traders before. You didn't give him any kind of warning, did you?"

"Okay, so I oversold the stock a bit. Everybody does it."

"Why did the deal with the Navy fall apart?"

"The app failed the final test. The stock tanked. Right into the crapper. Jim blamed me, but it wasn't my fault. My source flat-out lied to me. He knew all along the company couldn't deliver."

"Seriously?" Rick scoffed. "You expect me to believe someone inside the US Navy gave you a bogus stock tip so he could watch you lose money?"

"I ain't lying, man. Funny thing is, it wasn't me the guy wanted to get. It was Jim."

Rick laughed and shook his head. "Really. Who did this?"

"Heath Santiago."

Rick faced Monica, and they gaped at each other for a few seconds.

"The same Heath Santiago who is staying here?" Rick recalled his conversation with Alex. How she'd told him Santiago had been following Gordon's treasure-hunting activities for years.

"Heath wanted to destroy Jim," Brad said. "I only found out after this all fell apart. This deal nearly killed my business. The guy had thirty-five years in the Navy, man. He'd been in procurement for decades. Knew everything inside and out. I knew him, too. He was, like, the perfect source. And he burned me on our first deal. All because he had this hate thing going on with Jim. You want something good on Heath Santiago? Screw him. I can help you big time."

Rick raised one eyebrow and cocked his head to the side. If Brad wanted to talk, he was willing to listen. Rick snuck a sideways glance at Monica. She looked to be in shock. No worries, he thought. As long as she didn't interrupt.

"Go on." Rick had been in the same wet clothes for so long now they were actually starting to dry. Why bother changing now? He waited while Brad seemed to ratchet up his courage, but before he even started, Heath's door opened.

Heath's gaze flicked from person to person before settling on Brad. "I was on my way down to the wine tasting, but this looks pretty serious. What lies are you telling now, Brad?"

"No lies at all, Heath. Why don't you tell these two how you set up this entire weekend so you could destroy Jim?"

Heath watched Brad impassively, then turned to Rick and shrugged. "What of it?"

45

RICK

Heath Santiago stood stock still with his feet shoulder-width apart. His attitude. His posture. He looked as defiant as a man could get. But, this wasn't the Navy where he might have had some semblance of control over procedures. This was a murder investigation. And trying to stonewall wasn't going to fly. If Heath wanted to act tough, two could play. Rick held the man's gaze and didn't back away. "Are you admitting you set up this weekend?"

Heath spoke deliberately, apparently choosing his words with precision. "I did arrange it. I did not kill Jim. However, I wish I had. Someone else took away that final pleasure."

"So you came here intending to commit murder?" Rick asked.

"Yes."

"And you sent out the invitations?"

"Correct, again."

"I remember your registration. Your zip code is different from Cadman's, yet the invitations were postmarked with his."

"I rent a virtual office in Cadman's neighborhood. It was all quite simple, actually."

"So you wanted us to believe Cadman was the one who got everyone here."

Heath clasped his hands behind his back and waited, saying nothing.

"Well?"

"You haven't asked a question."

Rick was so tired of these jerks. "Stop playing games," he snapped. "Why did you let us believe Cadman arranged everything?"

"Because he's guilty," Brad said with a giant smirk on his face.

Rick cast a dirty look at Brad. "I asked him, not you."

"He doesn't bother me." Heath's voice held not a hint of emotion. "I knew sooner or later the truth would prevail. I'm a great believer in the truth coming out eventually. In my opinion, Cadman would never have gone to trial. And, as I said, my original plan was to murder Jim. Hence, I left a trail that led away from me. However, once he was dead—I realized someone had beaten me to the punch, and I had to remain silent."

"Would you have let Cadman go to jail?"

"I told you, it never would have gotten that far."

"Answer the question," Rick pressed. "Would you?"

"Cadman's not exactly the most innocent of people. He'll lead you to believe he's so pure, but he's got his share of skeletons."

"I don't care what he's done as long as it's not committing murder," Rick snapped. "But I have my answer about you." Whenever new guests arrived, they brought with them stories and excitement. What this group brought was pure antagonism. But, premeditated murder? That was on a whole different level.

"What about Hayden?"

Rick spun on his heel at the sound of the voice. Reese stood on the second-floor landing a few feet away glaring at Heath.

"What about him?" Rick asked.

"Don't you know? It's the boy's club. Right, Monica?"

"I...I don't know what you're talking about," she stammered.

"You're more obtuse than I thought." Reese turned her gaze to Rick. "Heath, Brad, Hayden, and Mark. They've been like a little club. I wouldn't be surprised if they didn't have a secret handshake. It was all part of beating Jim to the treasure, right Heath?"

"You're making it up as you go along." Heath shook his head. "Personally, I don't like these guys. And I sure didn't want to share anything with them. You could be right about the other three though." He shot a quick glance at Brad. "This one, Hayden, and Mark—kind of like the Three Musketeers."

Brad puffed himself up like a rooster preparing to enter a fight, but Rick motioned him to back off. "I get it. There's no love lost between any of you. But, you're not starting a fight in my B&B. I'll have you all thrown in jail."

"I don't tolerate insults." Brad glared at Heath. "Especially from skinny old geezers like him."

Heath took a small step forward and Rick stopped him with a hand on his chest. "He wants you to take a swing. Don't fall for it. He's a lot younger and stronger than you. Don't be stupid. Besides, I will call the cops no matter who starts a fight."

Running his tongue around the inside of his cheek, Heath seemed to settle down. It was becoming obvious that Brad had to be the "little birdie" Cadman referred to. Rick fixed a casual stare on him and waited.

"What?" Brad growled.

"So exactly how did you know where Cadman's monopod was in those rocks? When we searched the area, we didn't find it."

The color slowly drained from Brad's face while the others closed ranks around him.

To the side, Heath chuckled. "Looks like one of the musketeers has something to hide."

All Rick wanted to do was tell the idiot to shut up, but he held his silence, knowing anything he said might break the spell he now had over Brad.

"I can't believe that dirtbag talked," Brad said. "He was supposed to keep this between the two of us."

Rick wasn't about to correct the assumption. Best to simply let him think Cadman had ratted out his source. "What he didn't tell me was how you found out."

Brad screwed up his face for a second, then said, "It's all going to come out now. Hayden told me he saw Cadman taking photos. Later, when Jim was killed, I got worried for Cadman. You've seen how forgetful he is. Guy's got a memory like a sieve. That's all. I didn't want him to get in trouble."

"When was he taking these photos?"

"Last night. Sunset. According to Hayden."

"Before Jim was killed," Rick said.

"Well, hello, if he left it down there last night, the killer could have found it easily."

Not likely, thought Rick. Neither he nor Deputy Cunningham had found it during their search. "So you're assuming Cadman's monopod was the murder weapon."

"Uh, yeah, I guess so. Never really thought about it."

"That's BS, Brad, and you know it," Reese said. "Everything you do has a profit motive."

Rick had to agree. From what he'd seen, Brad didn't have an altruistic bone in his body. And he was obviously an accomplished liar. The only way to get the truth out of this jerk was to force it out. He'd talk to Hayden first, then circle back once he had something to use as leverage.

"We're not done," Rick said as he strode away. He also had a new theory to test. What if Cadman left the monopod in an obvious place and the killer moved it after murdering Gordon? At last, it was starting to feel like there was some traction. And a chance to change into something that didn't smell like fish.

46

RICK

Rick checked the time as he changed into a dry T-shirt and jeans. It was nearly four-thirty. Even Heath hadn't seemed in much of a mood to attend the wine tasting by the time Rick walked away from the conversation with the treasure hunters. Given the tense mood hanging in the air, it would probably be better if they didn't have anything to drink.

All the guests were told about the afternoon event when they checked in. Whether they attended was a completely different question. Rick stopped on the third step from the bottom of the stairs. Hayden was not only there, but appeared to have been doing a little sampling of his own.

His normally clear blue eyes were glassy and his five o'clock shadow was working overtime. He sat on one of the gray couches, wineglass in his hand, his laptop on the couch next to him.

Rick watched him for a few seconds. The man who had been so particular about precisely positioning his breakfast wore a T-shirt he hadn't tucked in completely. His head lolled in lazy circles as he contemplated the laptop screen. Could it be the murder? Or something else? Time to find out. Rick took the last three steps and tried to sound cheerful as he approached.

"Good afternoon, Mr. Kalstone."

"Afternoon," Hayden mumbled.

The hors d'oeuvres Marquetta had set up included several varieties of crackers and cheese. A bottle of Chardonnay and a half-empty bottle of Zinfandel were on the bar.

Without waiting for an invitation, Rick poured a taste of the zin into a glass and carried the bottle to the couch where Hayden sat. As if on autopilot, Hayden's glass came forward. Rick filled it, then offered a toast.

"To happier days."

"I'll drink to that." Hayden gulped down a mouthful of wine. "Where is everybody?"

Rick eyed his glass, wondering how Hayden hadn't heard the voices coming from the second floor. What the guy didn't know, he couldn't worry about. "Oh, I'm sure they'll be here soon. So you're a writer. What are you working on? Anything good?"

"It's always good with writers, except when it's bad." He gave Rick a drunken grin as he drained the last of his wine.

"I hear you. I've done a little writing myself." Rick filled Hayden's glass and indicated the laptop with a nod. "Is that your latest project?"

"I'm abandoning it. It was supposed to be this noir epic saga that spanned five generations. It reads more like a B documentary than fiction." He reached over and slammed the lid of the laptop. "Piece of crap."

"Have you written other books? I'll look you up."

"Nothing published yet. Too many competing projects. I get one thing moving, it stalls, and I'm on to something else."

"Well, let's not talk writing. You're the Vice President of this group. Impressive."

"Not so much. Nobody else wanted the job."

"Gotcha." Rick sipped from his glass. "Shame to waste a good zin. Last call. Let me top you off."

Hayden's expression glazed over as he swilled down his wine. He extended his hand for the refill.

"Good man," Rick said.

Now that Hayden was on his way to a full-blown drunk, Rick figured he wouldn't do well at lying. It was time to play a little game called Do You Remember What Lie You Told?

"I wish I was as good a photographer as Cadman is," Rick said. "There's a special bond between writers and photographers. Don't you agree?"

"No. Photography's not my thing. I have more appreciation for painters than shutterbugs."

"You're right, painting's a real talent. But, you've seen Cadman work, right? I understand you saw him taking photos down by the water."

"What are you getting at?"

Hayden's words slurred as he slumped to one side. If he listed much further, he was going to be sleeping on his laptop.

Rick raised the bottle and inclined his head toward Hayden. "Last call."

As Rick poured, Hayden asked, "Didn't we do last call already?"

"I won't tell if you won't." He winked, then raised his glass. "Salud!"

"Right on." Hayden knocked back another swallow.

"You told Brad you saw Cadman down there, right?"

A pair of vacant eyes peered back at Rick. It was as though the mind behind them wanted to focus, but couldn't. "What of it?"

"Oh, nothing. Nothing. I don't understand why you're involved with this group. A writer. Working on the great American novel. Doesn't that take up a lot of time?" Rick leaned forward and lowered his voice again. "I mean, everybody's got an angle. You have to be making money off this. How are you doing it?"

Hayden slouched down and smiled. It was one of those self-satisfied smirks, the kind most people shared only with a mirror. "Services, man. I sell services to treasure seekers." He snickered. "These people are so desperate they'll buy anything."

"Such as?"

"Oh, research. The secret to finding 'the big score.'" He emphasized the words with a bad falsetto, then snickered. "I've sold the same treasure hunter's guide a bundle of times. Even had maps to lost treasure." He laughed again. "It's the Gold Rush all over again. Everybody wants to be rich, but nobody wants to work."

Kind of like you, Rick thought. But, Hayden was way too drunk to be doing any introspection. "Nice business model. Did Jim know about it?"

His eyes drifted shut and Hayden arched his neck backwards. He breathed slowly with his mouth open. For a moment, Rick thought he'd fallen asleep, but when he looked at Rick again, the anger was obvious. "He knew about it. He called me out on it, too. The scum. The man never did a lick of research himself and he had the nerve to call me a fraud. Said I didn't believe in the cause. All he cared about was making money. It was all about the bottom line for him. I think the man bled green."

"Sounds like a good title for a book—The Man Who Bled Green. Catchy, huh?" It also sounded like Hayden might have a very good motive for murder.

"Yeah. Catchy." Hayden said, then swallowed more wine.

"Tell me something. If Jim called you a fraud, that must have irritated you to no end. Nobody likes that."

"Like I said, it was all about the money with him."

"At the expense of others?"

"Anybody and everybody."

"You included."

Hayden sighed and made an attempt to fix Rick with a stare. Whatever words he wanted to get out might be hopelessly lost in an alcohol-induced stupor. Rick hoped he hadn't given the man too much. He still had questions to ask. Especially the big one.

He leaned forward, shook Hayden's knee to be sure he was paying attention, then went for it. "So tell me, Hayden. Was Jim blackmailing you? How long had you been planning to kill him?"

47

RICK

Hayden peered at him in a way that gave Rick an odd sensation. Could it be the man actually understood the question and was willing—no, eager—to answer? It might have been the crooked smile—once again slightly sly and knowing. Or the way he deliberately set his wineglass on the coffee table and leaned back looking almost sober.

"I began planning to kill Jim after I learned what an evil man he was."

"Sounds like he hurt a number of people, including his ex-girlfriend and his former business partner," Rick said.

"He was a first-class jerk. I've been digging into his past for a long time." Hayden smirked. "I uncovered every little dirty secret of Jim's. The more I learned, the more I wondered—how would he react if he was dying?"

At breakfast, Monica had called Hayden their own Mr. Spock. He spoke with no emotion. His completely dispassionate expectation of perfection sent a chill down Rick's spine. Did he demand perfection from people, too? "Sounds very...logical. Are you a logical kind of guy, Hayden? Something's either right or wrong and there's no gray in between—is that you?"

Hayden's brief moment of clarity faded and he slumped back into the couch. "I like things done correctly. Precision is important. When something's broken, it must be repaired or removed."

"And did you remove Jim Gordon?"

"No." The answer came quickly and as casually as had his confession. "I never executed that part of my plan."

"Your plan? The one to murder Jim?"

Hayden massaged the back of his neck. His eyelids fluttered closed, then sprang open. "Someone beat me to it. The irony is, I never saw him die. All the planning, all the effort—all wasted."

"Wasted effort. Terrible thing for a perfectionist, right? What planning did you do?"

"So glad you asked. Don't tell anyone, but the map, that's my doing."

"You?" Rick gaped at him. Okay, he had not seen that coming. "It looks so...real."

Hayden sniggered and pinched his upper lip as his gaze wandered around the room. "I had the original designed by an art-history student I met at the UCLA Library. A hundred bucks. That's what it cost to create a freakin' work of art showing the location of the *San Manuel*." He chuckled again. "A measly hundred bucks."

"No way." Rick glanced around. They were still alone. He leaned forward and arched an eyebrow. "How'd you get it to look so old?"

"I began by staining the paper with tea, let it dry in the sun for couple of days, then buried it in the backyard for a week." Hayden chuckled and slapped his knee. "Nobody's figured out what I did."

Well, not exactly. Heath had. He'd confessed to sending the invitations. So how much had he known? "Pretty smart," Rick said. "Getting Jim to send it out—I'll bet that was tricky."

Hayden laughed again. "Jim didn't do that, man. Heath did. When I sold it to him for twice what I paid, he thought it was real. When I told him the thing was a fake, the guy got almost giddy. He was one of the victims of Jim's treachery, so he was more than happy to pay."

"What kind of treachery?"

"Heath has been beat out by Jim on various treasure hunts. Jim even stole his research once."

Rick nodded, the pattern of Jim Gordon's behavior emerging. "How did you make sure Heath didn't double-cross you?"

"He's not built that way. Did you know he was involved with Operation Rolling Thunder in Vietnam? That's what soured him on the whole establishment thing. He spent the remainder of his Navy career pushing paper and waiting for retirement. Guy who puts in that kind of time won't go back on his word. I thought about using his career as a plot for a novel, but the story never worked."

"You do a lot of plotting and planning, don't you?"

"I'm good at it."

"I can see that. You're the idea man."

"That's right," Hayden boasted. "I'm the man with the plan."

"But, Heath is the kind of man you admire, isn't he? Always keeps his word and he gets things done."

Hayden shrugged. "He does that, but admire?" He harrumphed. "Guy was useful cause he said he had a way to get rid of Jim. I told him I'd sell it to him, but I had to be there."

"I'll bet he paid for your room for the weekend. He did, didn't he?"

"Well, the map was worth more than two hundred to him. You gotta admit it's almost perfect. Work of art."

"Speaking of art, the tea you used to stain it, was it Darjeeling?"

Hayden's smug smile fell away. "How'd you know?"

"Our local stamp collector was sure it was a fake based on the paper. But it was my cook who nailed it. She recognized the floral aroma of the tea." Rick smiled at Hayden, who said nothing. "I was going to ask you why you used such a distinct tea, but that won't be necessary. You did it because you consider it close to a perfect tea and, if nothing else, you are a perfectionist."

Hayden scowled at Rick and remained silent.

"Tell you what, Hayden, I have to talk to Brad again. Why don't I help you up to your room so you can take a little nap? You're looking kind of under the weather."

Five minutes later, Rick was knocking on Brad's door. When there was no answer, he used his key and peeked inside. It appeared to be vacant. He entered the room, checked the closet and the dresser. Everything was gone. It was the same with the bathroom. He called Deputy Cunningham on his way down the stairs.

"Adam, I think Brad Luhan is trying to leave town. He's somehow tied into this." Rick pulled the registration card and relayed the particulars on the vehicle. He was still talking to Adam when he looked out the front window. Down the street, Brad was standing at the back of his blue Chevy. "He's still here. Make it quick."

"On my way."

The line went dead and Rick ran out the door, down the steps, and across the front yard to where Brad was parked. He arrived at the car just as Brad slammed the trunk.

"I thought Deputy Cunningham instructed everyone to stay in town, Brad."

"Something urgent came up."

Brad rushed to the driver's door, but the wah-wah of a police siren was already growing louder.

Rick raised his voice. "You've got to realize how bad this looks. Don't even think you'll escape."

Brad stood frozen in place as Adam's 4x4 pulled alongside. He cursed and hung his head. Slowly, he pulled the key from his pocket and returned to the rear of the car. He opened the trunk, pulled out his bag, and set it on the sidewalk.

He held up his room key. "Technically, I haven't checked out yet."

Rick glanced at Deputy Cunningham, who now stood outside his vehicle with his feet shoulder-width apart. He didn't look impressed.

"Mr. Luhan, do I need to take you in so you don't leave town?"

"I'm still here, Deputy. Didn't go anywhere and, like I said, I've still got my key."

"That's good," Rick said. "Because you forgot to mention a few things when we talked. And don't lie to me again. I've had enough for one day."

Brad stared at the sidewalk for a minute, then smiled. "I didn't lie to you, man."

With his frizzy hair, gold chain necklace, and nose ring, he reminded Rick of a hundred other snitches he'd seen over the years. He knew exactly how to handle him—instill fear. "It's called a lie of omission, right Deputy? And people go to jail for it."

Adam nodded and crossed his arms. Rick continued to stare down Brad, who gulped and finally muttered a weak okay.

"Good. And remember, as your buddy Heath so cleverly puts it, the truth will come out sooner or later. When that happens, you don't want to be on the wrong end. So tell us, other than Hayden, who else did you tell about the monopod? And how did you find out its exact location?"

48

RICK

Rick and Deputy Cunningham waited for a response from Brad, but when he remained unresponsive Rick's impatience boiled over. "I guess Brad doesn't want to discuss this any further. Maybe you should arrest him for obstruction."

The deputy rubbed his chin and did a visual assessment of Brad before answering Rick's question. "I hate paperwork. Unfortunately, some people don't realize the error of their ways until it's too late. Then they've got an arrest record."

"We can work this out. You don't have to bust me."

Rick pursed his lips as he peered at Brad. "Oh my gosh, Brad. Do you already have a record?"

"No, I don't, man. Honest."

"Guess there's only one way to be sure." Deputy Cunningham pulled out a pair of handcuffs and held them in plain view.

"Wait. Let's not get carried away, guys." Brad swallowed hard and his color faded. "I only told Mark how I saw the monopod down at the shore after Cadman was taking his stupid pictures."

"Where?" Rick demanded. "Exactly where did you see it?"

"By the sidewalk, man."

"The sidewalk? Not in the rocks."

"No, it was right there in plain view. I figured Cadman might be coming back for it."

"What else did you and Mr. Joshua talk about?" Deputy Cunningham asked.

"Not much that time, but after Jim got killed, we started kicking the idea around again. Mark kept going on about Cadman's mood swings, and so I got to thinking...what if Cadman was the murderer?"

"Why would you think that, Mr. Luhan?" Deputy Cunningham asked. His words hung in the air, the threat obvious—answer, or else.

"Because Cadman...he's a drug user, man. Mark told me the guy's hooked on oxy. Cadman could have killed Jim and wouldn't even remember it." Brad looked straight at Rick. "You saw it, right? At breakfast. That whole selective-memory-loss joke. It's for real, man. And it's because of the drugs."

Rick held up his index finger and narrowed his gaze at Brad. "How did Mark find out about Cadman's addiction?"

A cunning smile etched itself on Brad's face. "Hey, man, this is like my get-out-of-jail-free card, right?"

"This is your obstruction of justice charge if you don't talk." Deputy Cunningham moved closer to Brad, forcing him to take a step backwards.

"No worries, man. No worries. Mark is Cadman's dealer. I've never actually seen money, like, change hands, but there were signs."

"What signs?" Rick asked.

"On our first day here, Cadman had this wad of cash in his pocket. He was all fidgety and pacing around the lobby. It was like he was being secretive, you know?"

"I remember that," Rick said. He glanced at Deputy Cunningham. "I assumed he was the nervous sort. And he did keep pulling something out of his pocket. I never paid attention to what it was though. You talked to him at one point. What did you two say?"

"I asked him what was wrong, and he said it was none of my business. So, then I'm like, are you waiting for someone? And he's like, I've got a meeting with Mark. It seemed bogus, so I hung around and followed him when Mark checked in. They went into Mark's room and Cadman came out a few minutes later with a little paper bag. That's when I, like, made the connection. Mark's told me in the past he can get me prescription anything."

"He's telling the truth about following them," Rick said. "I saw him scuttling around."

"Scuttling, man? That's harsh."

Rick glared at Brad, who fingered his gold chain and quickly nodded his agreement.

"It's cool. No sweat, man. Scuttling it is."

Rick rolled his eyes and sighed. "We can ask Cadman. See if he remembers anything." By rights, they had plenty to corner and question Mark Joshua. But there had been so many lies told this weekend that Rick wanted some insurance. If he got lucky, this snitch might give it to him. "When you spoke to Mark, what exactly did he say?"

Brad stared off into space for a moment, then looked Rick in the eye. "Mark seemed all worried about someone finding Cadman's monopod. He didn't want the cops trying to pin that on his client. If Cadman goes away, Mark loses a payday."

"You still haven't answered me." Rick glanced sideways at Adam. "Don't make the deputy arrest you."

"No man, I was just thinking. You know, out loud. Anyway, what me and Mark kind of speculated was that Cadman...moved it. We agreed someone ought to tell him where it was—in case he wanted to get it back. That's all."

"Seriously? You thought he left his monopod down there, used it to commit murder, then stashed it ten feet from the body and forgot it was there? Are you kidding me?"

Brad licked his lips and fidgeted with the collar of his jacket. "Well, when you put it that way...but it makes sense if he's guilty. And neither of us wanted the murder pinned on him."

"Oh, for crying out loud, Brad. Why would you protect a man you don't even like?"

"Because...because the guy's had enough of a bad run," Brad stammered.

Rick felt a hand on his shoulder. It was Adam, quietly urging him to settle down. "You're right. Sorry." But deep down inside, Rick suspected the truth was finally coming out, and he wasn't about to let up the pressure on their reluctant snitch. "So what did you do? Run back to Cadman and squeal? You told him how the monopod was laying down in those rocks, didn't you?"

"Don't sound so cold, man."

"Answer the question," Deputy Cunningham snapped.

"I might've said something to him."

Rick heard Deputy Cunningham grunt in satisfaction. They exchanged a nod, and Rick said, "We may have our guy."

"What's that mean, man? You're not saying I killed Jim, are you? No way."

"No, Brad." Rick wanted to hold back the snarky remark, but couldn't. "I think you've been played for a patsy. Give me your car keys."

"Why?"

"So you aren't tempted to leave town again."

Rick waited, his hand out, until Brad glanced away. Adam stood to the side and indicated Brad should give up the keys with a silent nod.

"Fine. But don't drive it. Okay?"

Rick snickered as he pocketed the keys. "No worries, man."

Deputy Cunningham looked over his shoulder at his 4x4, then back to Luhan. "One last question. Where will we find Mark Joshua? Don't tell me he's decided to leave, too."

"Oh, Mark's not leaving. Not right away. He was going into town."

"Where?" Deputy Cunningham asked.

"I got no idea. Ask Hayden. He probably knows."

"Good grief, do you people ever stop?" Rick exploded.

"Stop what, man?"

"Lying," Rick sneered. "Let's go see Hayden—again."

Deputy Cunningham raised his eyebrows and looked at Rick. "Where do you expect to find him?"

"Hopefully, he's sound asleep." Rick gave Adam a sly smile. "He drank a little too much wine this afternoon."

"No issues I need to deal with?"

Rick shook his head. "Nothing to worry about. He was the only one at our wine tasting."

They found Hayden sound asleep in his room, and he wasn't at all happy about being woken up.

"What is wrong with this place? Can't a guy get some sleep around here?"

Deputy Cunningham showed Hayden his badge, who stared at it for a few seconds before appearing to recognize what it was.

"Sorry, Officer." His eyelids fluttered closed momentarily, then his eyes opened wide.

"Mr. Kalstone, I need you to answer a few questions. After that, you can go back to your nap and nobody will disturb you again. Okay?"

"Sure." The words came out slurred and were accompanied by a rolling of Hayden's eyes up to the ceiling.

Rick shook the man's shoulder. "Not yet, Hayden. Where's Mark Joshua?"

It took a moment for Hayden to process the question. When he seemed to understand, his brow furrowed. "Why are you asking me?"

"Because you two are best buds."

"Me and Mark? You kidding me? No way. It's straight-up business. Ask Cadman, he was looking for him, too."

"When was this?" Rick asked.

"A little while ago."

Rick gritted his teeth at how closely this investigation resembled being on a merry-go-round. They asked the obligatory question—where was Cadman. Of course, Hayden didn't know.

"Let's check his room," Rick said.

They knocked on the door to Cadman's room and received a response almost immediately.

"Give me a minute."

"Good. He's here," Rick said.

When the door opened, Cadman's face fell. "Oh, it's you. I thought—never mind."

"Who were you expecting? Mark?" Rick asked.

"Nobody in particular. What can I do for you?"

"Let's stop with the lies and evasive answers. Where's Mark Joshua?" Rick demanded.

Cadman sighed and hung his head. "It's all coming out, isn't it?"

"Your addiction, the lies about the monopod, yes, everything is coming out. Who were you expecting, anyway?"

"Brad. He called a couple of minutes ago. Said we had to talk."

"Mr. Richardson, I'm about one minute away from arresting all of you for the murder of Jim Gordon. You have that long to answer our questions."

The deputy flipped open his small pad and fingered his pen. It was obvious, at least to Rick, he was also tired of the runaround.

"What do you want to know?" Cadman massaged his forehead with his hand; his shoulders shook.

"What did Mr. Luhan want to talk about?"

"I don't know. That's the truth. He said you guys were getting close. I didn't understand what he meant by it so I told him to come on up."

Deputy Cunningham made a note before he glanced at Cadman. "Did you purchase oxycodone from Mr. Joshua?"

"Yes."

"Did Mr. Luhan tell you where to find your monopod?"

Cadman rolled his neck from side-to-side and his shoulders slumped. "Brad came to me and said he'd heard it was near where Jim died. He told me exactly where it was. He asked me if I was the killer and I denied it. But, the longer we talked, the more I realized what it would look like if someone found it. That's why I was down there. If you hadn't seen my flashlight none of this would have happened."

"Not quite," Rick said. "Jim Gordon would still be dead."

Deputy Cunningham asked, "Where is Mr. Joshua now?"

"He left to see the boat guy."

"The boat guy?" Rick asked. "You mean Joe Gray?"

"That's the one. He said they had some sort of business to conduct."

49

RICK

Rick and Deputy Cunningham drove to the harbor in the police 4x4. It would have been a little-boy fantasy come true with one exception. They decided to keep the lights and siren off to prevent Mark running at the sound of the approaching cruiser.

The back door of Joe Gray's houseboat stood open. Mottled sky reflected off the windows, giving them a faux-painted appearance. Roses and lavender in large pots lined the back end of the rear deck, which was a good ten feet from the dock. With each step on the dock's old planks, a few more creepy-crawlies inched up-and-down Rick's spine. One thing he knew for sure, he could have never been a cop.

"How do you do it, Adam?"

"Do what?"

"Stay calm in this kind of situation."

Adam snickered. "Who said anything about being calm? Right now, I feel like my blood pressure's through the roof." He took a deep breath and led the way onto the houseboat.

They both stopped and listened for a moment to voices coming through an open window. Rick said, "That's Mark talking to Joe. Doesn't sound like they're arguing or anything."

"Let's find out what arrangement these two have."

The deputy opened the front door and entered. Joe stood behind the counter, Mark in front. Joe smiled, quick and earnest. He waved a hand and invited the newcomers in.

"To what do I owe the honor, gentlemen?"

"Hey, Joe," Deputy Cunningham said. "We have a few questions for Mr. Joshua."

Rick kept a wary eye on Mark, who backed up as the deputy spoke. "Don't be trying to go anywhere."

"It's all good," Mark said. He leaned against the counter and raised his other hand. "Fire away."

The deputy asked, "What kind of work do you do, Mr. Joshua?"

"Excuse me? What's that got to do with anything?"

"Please answer the question."

"Whatever. I work in a hospital."

"Do you have access to prescription drugs?"

"No." Mark's fingers shook slightly as he stroked his beard and neck.

Recognition dawned on Joe's face and he narrowed his eyes. "What are we into here, Adam?"

Deputy Cunningham didn't look away from his suspect, and that seemed to make Joe even more uncomfortable. Now, he was also paying full attention to his supposed customer.

The deputy licked his lips. "I'm not quite sure yet."

Rick didn't like the way this was going at all. If Mark denied providing the drugs to Cadman, this would turn into a he-said, he-said contest. And Mark probably had his tracks covered.

"Were you renting a charter?" Rick asked.

"He was." Joe slid a piece of paper across the countertop.

Rick recognized the missing section of the treasure map immediately.

"How lucky can you get?" Joe said. "He found the—what the devil?"

Mark bolted through the open back door. Adam charged after him, but Joe hung his head and chuckled when they heard a loud splash and someone thrashing in the water.

"Could've told him you can't get out that way." Joe said. "Not unless he's a great jumper."

Joe sauntered to the door and peered out. Rick stood behind him. The deputy watched Mark tread water from the edge of the houseboat. Over his shoulder, he said, "Would one of you get me some rope or a pole to pull him out, please?"

"Sure thing, Deputy," Joe said as he reached to his right and handed Adam a long pole.

Once they had Mark out of the water, Joe brought a towel from inside and huffed. He muttered, "I just did the laundry yesterday."

As Mark dried off, the deputy began asking more questions. From the moment the interrogation started, it was obvious everything had changed.

"How did you meet Jim Gordon?" Deputy Cunningham asked.

"Through the San Manuel Society."

"How did you get the drugs you resold?"

"A nurse at work hooked me up with a supplier when I was injured. I discovered there was more money reselling oxy than working."

"Was Jim Gordon aware you were dealing?"

"Yes."

"Did he buy drugs from you?"

Mark laughed. "Are you kidding me? Straitlaced Gordon? He threatened to expose me if I didn't stop. For a guy who played so loose with the rules himself, you'd think he would have cut me a little slack. Not him. Not a chance. Gordon was one of those people who thought everybody else was put on this earth to serve his needs."

"So he wanted to do what? Have you arrested for dealing?" Rick asked.

Mark's face appeared to be lined with experience. Had he survived because of his wits? Brilliance? Neither mattered now. Apparently, he realized the same thing.

"Oh, why not? It's all falling apart and you guys will have enough to hang me. Maybe if I cooperate the judge will go easy." He gazed at Deputy Cunningham, who hadn't stopped scribbling notes, then to Rick.

Rick shrugged. "Worth a try."

"Yeah, worth a try." Mark snorted and ran a hand through his shock of wavy hair. "I've got nothing to lose. Jim made threats. All kinds. Told me if he ever saw me again, he'd call the cops."

"Was this at the B&B?"

"No. It was about a week before Heath sent the invitations. Should've seen the look Gordon gave me when we met. He wasn't expecting me, so he went ballistic when we ran into each other in the hall. Didn't say hello or screw you. The first words out of his mouth were, 'I'm done with you.'"

"I lied and told him I was only there for the treasure. I wasn't dealing anymore. He saw right through me. Asked me to go for a walk down to the shore. I was like, sure. Anything to salvage my life."

Deputy Cunningham was still writing in his notepad, so Rick decided he was free to ask any questions he wanted. "Is that how his body wound up on the rocks?"

"Call it a game of chicken that got out of hand. I guess he wanted to humiliate me or something because Jim climbed up on one of those rocks first and dared me to follow him. He said he'd let me off the hook if I showed him I had some guts. I looked down and saw Cadman's monopod. Right at my feet. Right by the pathway."

"He'd forgotten it when he left?"

"Must have. Anyway, I figured, his loss, my gain. I've used walking sticks before, so I extended it and joined old Straitlaced's little game. All of a sudden, Jim wasn't such a big man. He must've realized I had better balance and a weapon. He started backing up.

Almost fell and broke his neck once. I backed him up all the way to the edge. That's when I made him give me his copy of the map."

Mark laughed and a shiver ran through him. "I thought I had him. Beaten him on his terms. And then a wave hit him. The fear on his face when he fell into the water rear end first was priceless. Then he realizes how cold it is and the ocean's beating him up pretty good. After he smashed into the rocks a couple of times, he finally got it. He couldn't get out on his own. I considered leaving him out there. Just letting him die."

"But you didn't, did you?"

Mark's jaw quivered; his voice shook. "No. He begged me to help him. Promised to leave me alone. I wasn't sure I could live with myself if I walked away so I held out the monopod. He grabbed onto it. We got him back on land, and he started cursing at me again. He accused me of attempted murder. That was it. I'd had enough. Instead of the guy being thankful for saving his life, he wanted to make me pay even more. I still had Cadman's monopod in my hand. I can tell you one thing, the world's better off without him."

"One last question, Mark. What did you do with the monopod afterwards?"

"I started to throw it in the ocean, but I lost my balance and it landed in the rocks by accident. Hayden was coming, so I hid behind a big boulder and let him discover the body. As soon as Monica showed up, I joined them. I got worried someone would find the monopod, so I told Brad right where it was. I knew the little weasel would go straight to Cadman."

"One accident," Rick whispered.

"What's that?" Mark asked.

Deputy Cunningham gazed at him. "Rick?"

"Nothing. It's funny how quickly things can change." Rick shook his head. Mark Joshua's life had gone downhill all because he'd been injured in an accident. In some ways, he almost felt sorry for the guy.

Deputy Cunningham made one final note, then looked up from his pad. He glanced down at a small laminated card in his hand. "Mr. Joshua, I'm going to read you your rights. After that, you may want to call an attorney."

Rick stretched to relieve some of his pent-up anxiety. Somehow, it all seemed so anticlimactic. "If you don't mind, Deputy, I'll walk back to the B&B. I have a few things to sort out."

50

RICK

Rick didn't go straight home, but took a path through downtown. He barely noticed the tourists. Instead, he focused on the architecture. Along Main Street, old Victorian homes painted white with brightly colored trim had been converted to businesses. He passed the candle shop, the soap shop, and Scoops & Scones. He peered into windows, something he'd never really done. So many things he'd never noticed in this town. And now, he wanted to experience them all.

There was something else. For once, he felt connected to a place. To the people. Yes, even to those twenty-two mothers who wanted him to marry their daughters.

When he arrived home, he went straight to the kitchen, where Marquetta and Alex were standing at the center island. They each had a bath towel lying on the countertop in front of them. They'd rolled the ends to the middle so they formed two parallel tubes.

"Now, all we do is fold the towels over," Marquetta said. "Leave some room for the elephant's body, and the rolled parts create four legs."

Rick snickered. It really did look like an elephant's body—sort of. "So how do you make the head?" he asked.

Alex jumped up and ran to him. She grabbed his hand and pulled him to where her elephant body stood. "It's over," he whispered to Marquetta.

"I know," she said. "Adam called and said the guests could leave. Mr. Luhan and Miss Kelley checked out almost immediately. Mr. Richardson and Mr. Kalstone say they're staying until tomorrow morning." She grimaced. "Miss Potok will be with us for a while."

"She's a guest, that's all." Or were those simply words to make Marquetta and Alex feel better? If he were truthful, he still wasn't sure how he felt about Reese.

"Daddy, Marquetta's teaching me to make towel animals. We're doing an elephant now! Then we're gonna do a menu for a dinner party to benefit Robbie's family. We're inviting people so we can raise money to help them."

"It was all her idea." Marquetta gave Alex's shoulder a little squeeze and smiled at her.

"Marquetta told me about the accident Robbie's mom was in and I wanted to help out."

Alex rolled the corners of a hand towel into a triangle to match Marquetta's. They turned their towels over and pulled down the wide end. "This is the trunk," Alex said as she positioned her creation. She tilted her head to one side. "It looks funny cause he doesn't have any eyes."

Marquetta opened a wooden box which was filled with plastic baggies containing what appeared to be colorful eyes. Alex squealed and grabbed the one with blue eyes. "I'm gonna name her Ellie!"

What a delight it was to watch these two together. He hoped it would never end, and a fundraiser might be just what they needed. "What a great idea, Alex. Who are we inviting?"

"The whole town."

"So, this isn't just a way for me to meet the parents of my daughter's future husband."

"Daddy!" Alex said and hugged him.

Marquetta began to laugh. "Now I know you're a Planner. I've already been recruited to prepare the meal. And, Alex has talked to the florist about decorations."

Rick's vision blurred as he gazed down at his daughter. When he looked up at Marquetta, he whispered, "Thank you."

"You're welcome," she mouthed and swiped at her cheek.

There was a tug on Rick's waist. He looked down. Alex had one arm around him, the other around Marquetta's waist. He swallowed hard, content to enjoy the moment.

51

ALEX

June 17

Hey Journal,

Sorry I haven't written anything lately. It's been kinda crazy around here the last couple days. Mr. Richardson and Mr. Kalstone left yesterday. That Miss Potok is still here. She's been nice since Mr. Joshua got arrested, but I don't trust her. I bet she's trying to steal my dad away.

Me and Daddy and Marquetta are working on the dinner party for Robbie's family. So far, everybody we've asked has said they want to help. We've got flowers and candles and food and all sorts of stuff coming in. Marquetta says the tickets are selling like hotcakes.

I wasn't sure if Robbie would be cool with the whole dinner thing, but he's super excited. We're getting along better than ever. Daddy says I'm too young, but he's right. I'm gonna marry Robbie when we grow up.

xoxo,

Alex

PS I told Robbie about riding in the dumbwaiter. He doesn't want to do it cause he's afraid of getting in trouble again. But if I ask him real nice, he'll give in. I don't wanna make my dad mad again this week, so we'll wait. But we're totally gonna do it. It's gonna be awesome.

A TREASURE TO DIE FOR RECIPES

Here are recipes for the two breads in *A Treasure to Die For*. Feel free to print and share! I hope you love these as much as we did.

Converting these recipes to gluten-free is easy if you use a gluten-free one-to-one flour and gluten-free oats. We used Bob's Red Mill for both. These days, it's becoming much easier to find gluten-free baking ingredients, so there's no reason to not give gluten-free a try!

Chocolate Chip Gluten Free Banana Bread

We love quick breads like banana bread. But, sometimes we want them to be a bit different. The nice thing about this recipe is you can easily change things up. Don't want chocolate chips? Try pecans or walnuts, or raisins, or dried cranberries. The possibilities are limitless!

Prep Time: 20 minutes
Cook Time: 1 - 1/2 hours
Passive Time: 10 minutes
Servings: 1 loaf

INGREDIENTS
   1/2 cup unsalted butter softened
   1 cup sugar
   1 tsp vanilla extract
   2 eggs
   4 bananas ripe medium bananas peeled and mashed
   1 tsp buttermilk
   2 cups Bob's Red Mill Gluten Free 1-1 Baking Flour
(Can substitute all purpose flour if gluten-free is not needed)
   1 tsp baking soda

1 tsp ground cinnamon

1/2 tsp nutmeg

3/4 cup chocolate chips

INSTRUCTIONS

1. Preheat oven to 350 degrees.

2. Mix butter, sugar, and vanilla on high speed in mixer until creamy. The mixture should be light when done.

3. Beat in eggs, one at a time, until well blended.

4. Mash bananas with the milk in a separate bowl and set aside.

5. In another bowl, combine remaining dry ingredients.

6. Alternately mix about 1/3 of dry ingredients and 1/3 of bananas into the egg mixture until all are combined.

7. Bake for 1 - 1 1/2 hours. Check during last 1/2 hour for doneness by inserting toothpick or cake tester.

8. Allow to cool on wire rack for 10 minutes, then remove from pan and cool completely on wire rack.

RECIPE NOTES

There's a wide range of time for baking due to different baking speeds for different types of pans. Once you know how long your pan and oven take, you can lock that in as the baking time. Also, if you don't have a cake tester, just use a metal turkey lacer (it works really well!).

We found the original recipe listed below on FoodNetwork.com and did a little modification to make this breakfast bread gluten-free. At the same time, we added a little more spice. The result is a fabulous breakfast bread that is sure to impress anyone you serve.

Fresh Apple Oatmeal Breakfast Bread

A crumble topping adds flavor to this healthy Apple Oatmeal Breakfast Bread. Don't be scared off by the Xanthan gum ingredient. It's only needed with some gluten-free flours. If you use Bob's Red Mill 1-to-1 Baking Flour, you don't even need it.

Prep Time: 20 minutes
Cook Time: 1 hour
Passive Time: 10 minutes
Servings: 1 loaf

INGREDIENTS
Crumble Topping—
    1 teaspoon brown sugar
    3 tablespoons dry uncooked oats (use gluten-free, if desired)
    1/4 teaspoon cinnamon
    1 tablespoon melted butter

Bread—
    1 cup dry oats (use gluten-free, if desired)
    1 cup all-purpose flour (use gluten-free, if desired)
    Xanthan Gum Only needed for some gluten-free flours (Follow directions of flour package for correct amount!)
    1/2 teaspoon baking soda
    1/2 teaspoon baking powder
    1 teaspoon ground cinnamon
    1/4 teaspoon nutmeg

3 large eggs

1/4 cup honey

1/3 cup vegetable oil

1 teaspoon vanilla extract

1/3 cup brown sugar

2 cups unpeeled shredded apples (2 large apples should do the trick)

1/2 cup chopped walnuts

INSTRUCTIONS

1. Combine brown sugar, oats, cinnamon and melted butter in a small bowl. Set aside.

2. Preheat oven to 350 degrees. Cut a piece of parchment paper large enough to just cover the base of the bread pan. Place in bottom of the pan. Grease the parchment paper with butter or use a cooking spray.

3. Place oats in a blender and process to a flour-like consistency.

4. In a large bowl, combine oats with next four dry bread ingredients (all purpose flour, baking soda, baking powder, and cinnamon).

5. In a medium bowl, combine eggs, honey, oil, and vanilla.

6. Stir brown sugar into egg mixture until combined. Add in apples and stir again. Slowly add in flour mixture, being sure to not over-mix. Gently stir in walnuts.

7. Pour batter into the loaf pan and sprinkle with crumble topping.

8. Bake for 1 hour or until a wooden toothpick (or a cake tester) comes out clean when inserted. Cool on wire rack for 10 minutes, then remove from pan and cool completely on wire rack.

BEHIND THE STORY

There was a time in college when I thought I wanted to be an archaeologist. When it actually came time to find a job where I could use my BS in Anthropology, I discovered finding a job was a lot harder than getting a degree. I wound up chasing deadbeats for a living, which was a far cry from digging up artifacts. Fast-forward many years and my inner-archaeologist surfaced in the little town of Seaside Cove.

Archaeology, however, is based on fact, not fiction. So let's start by separating the facts from the fiction. The legend of the *San Manuel* as relayed by Rick to Francine in Chapter 6 is a complete fabrication. The Manila Galleons came into existence in the mid 1560s. The ships sailed from Acapulco, which was a part of New Spain, to the Philippines using a southern route. They returned via a northern route which took four to eight months and was one of the most treacherous journeys known at the time.

The facts were accurately described by Reese in Chapter 27 during her conversation with Joe Gray. The returning Manila Galleons did carry Far East products such as spices, porcelains, silks, and ivory. There were ships lost at sea due to a variety of hazards including privateers and bad weather. While few ships are known to have sunk off the California coast, there are still some unaccounted for. With their cargos worth millions, perhaps billions, of dollars, is it any wonder we all love to fantasize about lost treasure?

One final note on treasure. A billion dollars is not an unrealistic estimate for the value of a galleon's salvage. The *San Jose*, which was discovered off the coast of Cartagena, Columbia, is estimated to have a value well in excess of a billion dollars.

The recipes for this book are also available on my website at http://terryambrose.com/treasure-die-recipes/. You'll be under no obligation to leave an email address or any other personal information.

ABOUT THE AUTHOR

Once upon a time, in a life he'd rather forget, Terry Ambrose tracked down deadbeats for a living. He also hired big guys with tow trucks to steal cars—but only when negotiations failed. Those years of chasing deadbeats taught him many valuable life lessons such as—always keep your car in the garage.

Today, Terry likes fast, funny mysteries and cool photography. When he's not writing, he's out looking for that next amazing photo to share. Find him at terryambrose.com.

52482832R00138

Made in the USA
Columbia, SC
03 March 2019